MW00694974

DOCTOR WHO
THE CHASE

DOCTOR WHO
THE CHASE

based on the BBC television series by Terry Nation
by arrangement with BBC Books, a division of
BBC Enterprises Ltd

JOHN PEEL

Number 140 in the
Target Doctor Who Library

A TARGET BOOK

published by
the Paperback Division of
W H Allen & Co Plc

A Target Book
Published in 1989
By the Paperback Division of
W H Allen & Co Plc
Sekforde House, 175/9 St John Street,
London EC1V 4LL

Novelization copyright © John Peel, 1989
Original script copyright © Terry Nation, 1965
'Doctor Who' Series copyright © British Broadcasting
Corporation, 1965, 1989

The BBC producers of *The Chase* were
Verity Lambert and Mervyn Pinfield
The director was Richard Martin
The role of the Doctor was played by
William Hartnell

Printed and bound in Great Britain by
Courier International Ltd, Tiptree, Essex

ISBN 0 426 20336 4

This book is sold subject to the condition that it shall
not, by way of trade or otherwise, be lent, re-sold,
hired out or otherwise circulated without the
publisher's prior consent in any form of binding or
cover other than that in which it is published and
without a similar condition including this condition
being imposed upon the subsequent purchaser.

Contents

Author's Note

This book is not strictly an adaptation of the televised version of *The Chase*. It follows, for the most part, the original scripts for the show, as written by Terry Nation. As is the case with most series, the original scripts were rewritten for various reasons – to make scenes less expensive, to perform the actions in a simpler way, or to add character touches to the story. In the case of *The Chase*, the changes made from Terry's original scripts were sometimes quite extensive.

Faced with the task of novelizing either Terry's scripts or the televised ones (presumably the changes having been made by then-story editor Dennis Spooner), I have in most cases opted to stay with Terry's versions. There are two main reasons for this. Firstly, the original scripts delve more deeply into the alienness of the creatures that the Doctor and his companions meet. On the television, a lot of this was cut simply because it would have been too expensive to film. In a book, I am under no such constraints. Secondly, the television version of *The Chase* exists in its entirety, and may some day be seen again by British audiences. (American viewers are better off, since they have the story in their syndication package.) Thus, it seemed to me to be more interesting to novelize the scripts that cannot be seen.

However, I did elect to retain certain sequences that exist in the filmed version of the tale and not in Terry's scripts. I also made a number of changes in the *Mary Celeste* sequence, to fit the final novel into the known facts about that most mysterious of ships. Readers with enquiring natures can find an excellent account of the facts in *Mystery Ship*, written by George S. Bryan, and published by Lippincott in 1942.

Finally, this note would not be complete without mention of Kate Nation – Terry's wife – who unearthed the original scripts for us; and of Nan – my wife – who read and made relevant comments and suggestions throughout the work. Accordingly, it is to these two ladies that this book is dedicated. Without their help and encouragement, life would be considerably more complex and less enjoyable.

1

The Executioners

The room had a background pulse, like an electronic heart slowly beating. The lighting was subdued, too dim for human eyes. There were no human eyes present, merely the computer-augmented lenses of the Dalek monitoring staff, and that of the Black Dalek. On an elevated ramp, it moved backwards and forwards, slowly and patiently, its eyestick turned to survey the instruments in the pit below. Flickering lights played across the many instruments and sensors, though none in the pattern that the Black Dalek's inbuilt computer was waiting for.

Finally, the screens lit up with an electric-blue pattern, shifting and changing, spiralling inwards on the main monitor. The Chief Scientist spun around. 'The enemy time machine has been located,' it reported formally, though the Black Dalek was already aware of the fact.

'Location?'

'It has just left the planet Xeros,' the scientist answered. 'Our projections place its next destination as the planet Aridius.'

'Acceptable,' the Black Dalek replied – its highest compliment. 'Order the special squad to assemble in the Project Room.'

'I obey!'

The Black Dalek moved out of the room, heading for the Project itself. Years of planning were finally reaching the day of action. For decades, the Daleks had been balked in their plans to expand and take their rightful place as the masters of the Universe – chiefly through the activities of a single being. Now, however, the balance would be restored, and their greatest enemy would be destroyed. Ahead of the Black Dalek, a door slid open, and it entered the special Project Room. An elevated ramp allowed it to look down at the featureless box in the centre of the room. This stood some eight feet square, with a door on what was obviously the front. Nothing else marked it as being the single greatest achievement of Dalek technology.

Below the ramp, another door opened, and the special team entered, to form a precise line in front of the box. Their eyesticks raised to face the Black Dalek, expectantly.

'Our greatest enemy has been located,' it informed them. 'His location is being programmed into your instrumentation. Your instructions are to follow – locate – and destroy!' It turned to trigger the large monitor screen on the far wall. It sprang to life, showing what appeared to be a London Police Box of the 1960s. 'The TARDIS!' the Black Dalek exclaimed.

''TARDIS!!' the assembled Daleks echoed.

'Our enemy is the Doctor. His appearance has changed many times over the years, yet our instruments have determined his basic metabolic pattern. This has been programmed into your computers. You are to locate and exterminate him. *Exterminate*!'

'Exterminate!'

With satisfaction, the Black Dalek watched as its Daleks filed into their own time machine. Shortly after the final one had entered, there was a strange, electrical tension in the air. With a rush of wind, the box vanished.

The executioners were on their way to intercept and destroy the Doctor. The Black Dalek paused for a short while, then turned and left the room. It would wait in the monitoring room for the inevitable report that the Doctor had been exterminated.

2

A Speech in Time

The Space/Time Vortex exists outside of any normal frame of reference. Within it, light, darkness, matter and energy all blend, divide, shift and change. It underlies the whole of Creation, touching the normal Universe only slightly. Its pathways are twisted, unstable and hard to follow. A journey through these strange dimensions might take a moment and carry a traveller a million years and a billion light years from his/her/its origin. Alternatively, a journey of months in the Vortex might end in a shift of six feet and ten days in conventional space. Without being able to calculate the pathways, there was simply no telling.

The TARDIS ploughed through the Vortex without any kind of plan. It was a time and space craft whose exterior belied its sophisticated construction. It looked like a Police Box on the outside, but within its apparently cramped confines lay a huge, technologically advanced craft. It was quite capable of choosing any of the myriad paths through the Vortex and passing along them – provided the navigator knew what he was doing. In this case, the navigator was known simply as the Doctor. He had very little knowledge of what he was doing in terms of guiding the ship. He had simply – well, he liked to call it 'borrowed', but other people have stronger and blunter words for it – the craft. He had lost the operational notes he had taken some years before in the prehistoric dawn of the age of man on Earth. As a result, the TARDIS simply followed the shifts and changes of the Vortex wherever they might lead.

The Doctor was not at all bothered by such random

wanderings. He was getting on a bit in years – almost 750 by now – but had not yet undergone his first regeneration. His body was a bit worn – thin, aged ('matured' was the word that he preferred), and with a mane of flowing white hair. He had developed a number of traits that marked him indelibly in people's memories – brusqueness, self-congratulation and irritability being among his good points.

This was the third day of the current trip (all time being measured from the stately ormolu clock in the control room), and the inhabitants were getting rather bored. Ian Chesterton – one-time science master of Coal Hill School – sat reading in an elegant Queen Anne chair. A tall, handsome and well-built man in his mid-thirties, he had undergone many changes from teacher to a seasoned traveller in time and space. He was now quite absorbed in his book, however, much to the annoyance of Vicki.

She was the latest member of the TARDIS travelling party, having been rescued from a crashed spaceship on the planet Dido, some time in the twenty-fourth century. Vicki was a healthy, cheery teenager, and had accompanied the travellers expecting excitement and adventure. Three days of being cooped up in the TARDIS were driving her crazy. She was, after all, still a typical teen – whatever century she was born in – and she hated doing nothing. Peering at Ian, she asked, 'Is it good?'

'Mmm?' Ian, still engrossed in the story, looked up. 'Not bad. Bit far-fetched.' Then he went back to reading. Vicki glanced at the title, *Monsters From Outer Space*, with its lurid illustration of a multi-tentacled alien attempting to clutch a virtually naked woman. The things he read! Still, he was too absorbed to pay her any attention, so Vicki wandered off through the doorways and into the activity room.

Barbara Wright was in there, working away with scissors on a dress. She was a pretty, strong-willed and capable woman of about thirty and had once been the history teacher in the same school as Ian. Both had followed their mysterious pupil, Susan, back to her home one night. They had stumbled into the TARDIS and been whisked into a journey stranger than even Scheherazade could have told. Susan had been left on the Earth of the future to marry the man she had fallen in love with. It had been hard for the Doctor to abandon her, but he seemed to have taken Vicki into his heart as a surrogate grand-daughter in Susan's place.

'I,' Vicki said, striking a dramatic pose in the doorway, 'I am a useless person.'

'Mnnsnsn,' Barbara muttered, and then removed the dressmaking pins from her mouth. 'Nonsense,' she repeated. 'Come and give me a hand.'

'What are you doing?'

'Adapting some of Susan's clothes to fit you. You can't wear one dress forever, you know – even if it is dirt-repellent and self-cleaning.'

'Do you think Susan would mind?' To be honest, Vicki had been getting bored wearing the same outfit constantly.

'I'm sure she won't. Come over here and put this on. Let's see how well I've—'

Whatever she might have said was totally lost in an incredible ear-splitting whine that came from nowhere. Both of them slapped their hands over their ears in agony, wincing in pain. They ran into the control room, to find Ian likewise in agony, and staring at the Doctor.

Giving the Doctor time to tinker about in the TARDIS was always dangerous, but he had seemed to be happily absorbed in the harmless activity of working on a machine he had dragged out of the TARDIS laboratory. It was basically a screen surrounded by a complex array of instrumentation. A pile of plastic cards lay scattered about it, and the terrible whine was coming from the speaker mounted just above the screen. Ian rushed over, only to be pushed rudely aside by the Doctor, who was armed with a large screwdriver, and intent on attacking further controls.

'What's the matter with it?' Ian yelled at the top of his voice.

'What?' the Doctor howled back. Then he shrugged, and turned his attention to the device. After a moment of concentration, he applied the screwdriver, twisted, and the howl died out. His three companions shook their heads to clear the lingering effects of the noise and sighed.

13

'I asked what the trouble was,' Ian said. 'Are you trying to deafen us, Doctor?'

'Deafen?' the Doctor echoed, as though the possibility had never occurred to him. 'No, no, no, no, no, dear boy. Just an unfortunate juxtaposition of the sonic rectifier and the lineal amplifier.' He stared at the machine again, like a lion-tamer in a cage of hungry carnivores.

'Oh, of course,' Ian muttered, sarcastically. 'I should have known at once.'

Barbara was staring at the machine in fascination. The TARDIS was so vast, and so cluttered with the junk that the Doctor had accumulated, that she had no idea what the device might be. 'Just what *is* this, Doctor?'

Muttering to himself about work never getting done, the Doctor turned around. 'I *told* you,' he exclaimed, though he had not. 'It's a space/time visualizer.'

Staring dubiously at it, Barbara pressed her luck. 'Apart from making that terrible noise, what does it do?'

The Doctor tucked the screwdriver absentmindedly into an inside pocket, then gripped his shabby coat's lapels. Striking his stance as a lecturer, he informed her: 'It taps into the continuum of the Space/Time Vortex, converting the photons there into electrical impulses.'

'Oh, good,' Ian enthused. 'I've always wanted one of those.'

'Do I detect a note of sarcasm, Chesterton?' the Doctor demanded haughtily.

Trying to stave off an argument, Ian apologized quickly. 'I'm sorry, Doctor, but you rattle off explanations that would have baffled Einstein, and expect us to know what you're talking about.'

Muttering something about small minds of human beings, the Doctor decided he had better explain or he'd never get any peace. 'Oh, very well. Have you heard of Venderman's Law? "Light has mass and energy intermixed, therefore—" '

'—therefore energy radiated by photons and tachyons is equal to the energy absorbed,' Vicki finished.

'Splendid, child, splendid,' the Doctor approved. 'It's nice to find one sharp mind at least.' He glanced pointedly at Ian and Barbara.

14

'It's quite simple, really,' Vicki interposed. 'It just means that anything that happened anywhere in the Universe exists as light particles within the Space/Time Vortex and can theoretically be reconstructed electronically.'

The Doctor beamed at her. 'Couldn't have put it better myself.'

Vicki started to look over the Visualizer in fascination. 'You know, when I left Earth, scientists were trying to invent a machine to tap into the Vortex and record the patterns there. Then we could just tune in and witness any event in history!'

'And that's exactly what this does,' the Doctor finished for her, with a certain amount of what he felt was justified pride.

'A sort of . . . time television!' Barbara exclaimed.

'Precisely.' Having established his superiority, the Doctor was quite magnanimous. 'I'll give you a demonstration. Chesterton – think of an event in history.'

Ian laughed. 'All right.' He thought a moment. 'Now, what do you need to know?'

'First of all the planet.'

'That's easy – Earth.'

The Doctor moved to the control panel, and began adjusting the controls. Having punched in a long code, he picked out one of the plastic cards, and inserted it. 'Now the time and as accurate a location as you can manage.'

'Pennsylvania, USA,' Ian said firmly. 'November 19th 1863.'

Nodding, the Doctor worked further controls. The screen came to a flickering life, as the Doctor adjusted the settings. Finally, it came into a burst of colour, and the picture focused. The three onlookers leaned over the hunched back of the Doctor, staring at the screen. It was as if a camera were zooming through narrow streets of wood-built houses, until it narrowed on to a field. There was a rough platform, on which a tall figure stood. Behind him stretched marker after marker in neat order. Before him, a crowd of people waited expectantly. The picture settled on the man, and his familiar features clarified.

'Fourscore and seven years ago,' Abraham Lincoln began, slowly, clearly, sonorously, 'our fathers brought forth on this continent a new nation, conceived in liberty and dedicated to the proposition that all men are created equal.'

Ian and Barbara looked at one another, astounded. Vicki glanced at the Doctor, impressed. The Doctor, naturally, gripped his lapels and looked rather smug.

'That's – Abraham Lincoln!' Barbara exclaimed.

'That's what I asked for,' Ian laughed, not quite believing it. 'The Gettysburg Address.'

Unconscious of these strange watchers, Lincoln continued. 'Now we are engaged in a great civil war, testing whether that nation or any nation so conceived and so dedicated can long endure. We are met on a great battlefield of that war . . .'

The time travellers watched, with rapt attention, through to the end of Lincoln's speech.

'It is for us to be rather here dedicated to the great task remaining before us – that from these honoured dead we take increased devotion to that great cause for which they gave the last full measure of devotion; that we here highly resolve that these dead shall not have died in vain; that this nation, under God, shall have a new birth of freedom; and that the government of the people, by the people, for the people shall not perish from the Earth.'

Lincoln paused, his speech over. Thunderous applause greeted him from the assembled crowd, as the Doctor adjusted the controls, and the picture faded away. There was silence a second, then Barbara pressed forward. 'Can I choose something, Doctor?'

'And me!' Vicki exclaimed. 'Please – can I?'

Smiling benevolently, like Santa at Christmas, the Doctor nodded. 'All in good time, all in good time. You can both have a turn. Come along, Barbara – you watched me at the controls. Now you select a slice of history for yourself.'

Barbara bit her lip, concentrating, then moved forward to manipulate the instrumentation. 'There is something I've always wanted to know,' she said, wistfully.

'Oh?' Ian leaned over her shoulder. 'What?'

'Come on,' Vicki laughed. 'Tell us!'

Barbara pulled a face. 'You'll see in a minute.' She pressed the actuator, and all eyes turned to the screen. The interference cleared, and a picture began to form. It seemed to focus on a window, then pull back. About the leaded glass was highly polished wood. As the picture clarified, it revealed a tall, thin man in Elizabethan costume. He was staring at a second, more rotund figure in disgust, as if he had been some insect crawling over the floor. The picture was finally complete as it also included a stately woman on a throne. She was obviously past her best, her skin powdered a pure white, her hair a hennaed red. This was clearly none other than Queen Elizabeth the First. She regarded the portlier man with some degree of hauteur.

'Master Shakespeare,' she said, coldly. 'Many people have been talking of your latest play. They tell me that your figure of Falstaff is based on none other than Sir John Oldcastle.' After a short silence, she prompted, 'Well?'

The playwright took a deep breath, wondering what his chances were of living to pen another line. Finally, he decided that perhaps telling the truth was his best course. 'Ah, yes, your majesty, he is.'

'Aha!' Elizabeth exclaimed, glaring triumphantly at Sir Francis Bacon. 'I thought so. Well, pay it no further mind. I myself have an excellent idea of the subject for your next play.'

Shakespeare was caught between relief that he had been let off so lightly and apprehension that he would be strictly told what to write in future. 'And – ah – what might that be, most gracious lady?'

'You shall write,' the Queen began, and then paused, dramatically, 'of – Falstaff in love.'

His smile definitely forced, Shakespeare bowed. 'An . . . excellent idea, your majesty.' He started to retreat, only to run into Francis Bacon behind him. The two men left the room, and Shakespeare felt Bacon's hand on his shoulder.

'I, too, have an idea that you might wish to use,' Bacon said.

Was there no end to this? Shakespeare took a deep breath. 'Indeed?'

'Have you heard of the history of Hamlet, prince of

Denmark?' Bacon sounded as though he had discovered the Holy Grail.

Shakespeare sniffed, loudly. 'Not my style at all, I assure you,' he said quickly, and then left.

Bacon stared at the open door in disgust. 'Scribbler!' he snarled in contempt, and turned back to the court.

Outside, Shakespeare paused, in thought. 'Hamlet,' he mused. 'Then again . . .'

The picture broke up. Ian laughed, and put his arm round Barbara's shoulder. 'Is that what you wanted to know?'

'I'm not sure. I only wondered if Shakespeare had really written his own plays, or if Bacon had been their real author. It was a chance to find out for certain what literary scholars have argued over for centuries.'

None of this mattered to Vicki, who cared nothing for plays or poetry. Instead, now that it was definitely her turn, she dived for the controls and began to manipulate them. Finally, she grinned in satisfaction. The other three turned with her to watch her choice on the screen.

It was clearly some sort of a television programme that Vicki had tuned into. Judging from the clothes, it was from the 1960s. Barbara felt a strong twinge of homesickness. One man, with a microphone, smiled professionally at the cameras. 'Ladies and gentlemen,' he announced, 'the . . . fabulous . . . Beatles!'

The camera switched to the famous foursome, which immediately broke into a song that neither Ian nor Barbara recognized. It was 'Ticket to Ride', written two years after the teachers had been snatched away in the TARDIS by the Doctor. By the look on Vicki's face, though, she recognized the tune – and seemed somewhat disappointed.

'Don't you like the Beatles?' Ian asked.

'What? Oh, yes, they're good. It's just that . . . well, I didn't know that they played *classical* music!'

'Classical?' Barbara spluttered.

Ian raised an eyebrow. 'Get with it, Barbara – times change, times change.' He couldn't help laughing at the expressions on both of their faces. 'I'll bet that by Vicki's time they're into something *really* weird and calling it music!'

18

Before either of them could respond to this cheek, a loud tone from the mushroom-like control panel brought them round. Vicki's hands caught the settings on the Visualizer, and the picture faded.

The Doctor, the episode with the Visualizer now forgotten, moved towards the panel. 'We're landing,' he announced. Barbara and Ian could not help looking at one another in a mixture of hope and worry. Where in all of time and space were they going to appear?

3

The Sands of Death

The scanner showed nothing but sand and rocks in all directions. The sky held two suns, which immediately dashed any hopes that the TARDIS had stumbled back on to the Earth again. The sky was completely devoid of clouds, and the whole place looked totally lifeless. After a few more minutes fussing with the controls, the Doctor looked up.

'Everything's perfectly all right,' he announced, cheerfully. 'Oxygen a bit high, gravity a little greater than on Earth.'

'It looks hot,' Barbara observed.

'And small wonder,' the Doctor replied. 'Those twin suns are very close, cosmically speaking.'

Ian was in good humour. 'Just right for a day on the beach, eh?'

'As long as you don't go looking for the water,' the Doctor quipped back. 'I think it's safe to go out.' He opened the doors, and led the way. Ian lingered to put on a flashy-looking blazer; might as well look the part of a day tripper, he decided.

Outside, the heat would have been oppressive, had the air not been so dry. It did indeed seem like a day at the beach. Vicki, ever impatient, asked: 'Are we going to explore?'

Not fancying a walk in this heat, Barbara said dubiously, 'Doesn't look like there's much here.' Shading her eyes against the glare, she looked about. 'Just miles and miles of sand.'

Facts weren't enough to dampen Vicki's enthusiasm. 'But you don't know that *for sure*,' she cajoled. 'I mean . . . just over that sand dune over there might be a city – or a space station – or, or *anything*!'

Affectionately, the Doctor patted the teenager on her shoulder. 'Always have to know what's on the other side of the hill,' he smiled. 'Well, go along child. I don't see what harm you can come to.'

'Aren't you coming?'

'No, no, no, no, no. I'd find walking in all this heat a little strenuous.' He glanced around at Ian. 'Chesterton, you go with her.'

Laughing at the Doctor's attempts at avoiding exercise, Ian agreed. 'All right,' he told Vicki in mock tones of severity, 'but only to see over the next ridge.'

'Of course,' Vicki promised, in a tone that suggested nothing of the kind. She grabbed his hand, bursting with energy now that they were free of the TARDIS again. 'Come *on*!'

'I'll stay with the Doctor,' Barbara said, before she could get invited along on this little trip. Ian laughed, and then gave in to Vicki's insistent pulling, and set off with her.

The Doctor chuckled to himself, then returned to the TARDIS. In a moment, to Barbara's surprise, he returned with two deckchairs. 'May as well enjoy the sun,' he suggested. Barbara accepted a chair gratefully, noticing that it had 'Blackpool Beach' stamped on it. As she settled down in it, she idly wondered what the fines on a chair several hundred – or million – years overdue were . . .

Vicki had already made a find. She was kneeling beside a peculiar stain on the sand as Ian caught up with her. 'Over here,' she called. 'Look at this.' The stain glistened wetly, a dark-red colour. She touched it, and it felt warm and slimy. 'Ugh.'

Ian crouched beside her. 'What is it?'

'I don't know.' She looked up, scanning the sands. 'There's more of it over there . . . and beyond that. It's like a sort of trail.' She rose to her feet, and Ian stood too.

'I think it's blood of some kind,' he announced, grimly. So this world wasn't lifeless, after all. 'Let's just take a look where it leads – but any sign of trouble, and we go back.'

Nodding, Vicki started along the pathway of – blood? Ian, still disturbed by this, moved after her. He would have been even more disturbed had he glanced back.

By the stain, the sand was shifting slightly, stirred from below. Slowly, something began to emerge from under the surface, rising vertically. It was a dark, sandy colour, like the stem of a large plant. In its tip, however, was a multi-faceted eye which stared after the two figures that plodded off into the dunes . . .

Barbara rolled over slightly, luxuriating in the warmth of her skin. It seemed to her that far too few of the planets they visited were as peaceful as this. No monsters, no alien menaces, no running for their lives, no getting involved in a history that had once only been preserved in books for her – just relaxing in the sun. 'I suppose with two suns I'll get brown twice as quickly,' she murmured.

The Doctor wasn't listening. Instead, he was letting sand slip through his fingers, enjoying the warmth. Somewhere in the back of his mind, he recalled a time like this when he had been young, many centuries ago. He had learnt a song – had been rather good at it, as he remembered. The words came back now, and he started to sing it softly to himself, quite content and at peace with everything.

An electronic whine roused Barbara. Sitting up, she asked, 'What's that awful noise?'

'Mmm? Awful noise?' His mood broken, the Doctor sat up, indignant. 'Not a nice thing to say about my singing!'

'No, not *that* awful noise,' Barbara said without thinking. 'The other one. Listen . . .' They both paused, and could hear the whining sound.

'Oh, yes, yes,' the Doctor sighed. 'In all the excitement of landing, Vicki must have left the Visualizer on. Barbara, my dear, would you switch it off? Mmm? Thank you.'

That was typical of the Doctor, Barbara knew – blame Vicki first for leaving on his latest toy, then try and flatter her into turning it off. She rose to her feet, knowing that she'd better turn it off; it was obvious that the Doctor aimed simply to laze about.

Watching her enter the TARDIS, the Doctor settled back, and started to hum to himself. 'Awful noise indeed,' he muttered. 'Huh! I could charm nightingales out of the trees with my voice in my youth . . .'

Inside the TARDIS, Barbara crossed to the Visualizer. The screen was showing broken images, the speaker making this terrible humming. None of the controls was set, and it was simply tuning in to the random pathways of the Vortex. Realizing that the Doctor hadn't told her where the off-switch was, she began to hunt for it. While she did so, the images on the screen began to resolve themselves, tapping into the latest disturbances in the ether. The first Barbara knew about it was when the speaker stopped humming, and instead a terrible, familiar voice issued from the box.

'The Dalek Prime is ready to receive your report!'

Barbara stared at the screen in terror. She saw the Black Dalek glide through a doorway into a large laboratory. Within was a Dalek that was larger than most, and painted a uniform golden colour. Behind it were panels of screens, mounted from floor to ceiling, from wall to wall. There must have been a hundred of them, and all showed exactly the same picture – the TARDIS in the very desert where it now stood. 'Doctor!' she yelled. 'Doctor! Come quickly!'

The Black Dalek drew to a halt before the Dalek Prime. The room contained several other Daleks moving about and clearly hard at work – but at what? 'The report is ready,' the Black Dalek intoned.

Entering through the door, the Doctor was wiping his brow with a large handkerchief. 'What is it?' he asked, irritably. 'Can't I relax for even . . .' He stopped dead as he saw what was on the screen. 'Daleks!' he spat.

The Dalek Prime finally spoke.

'Give your report.'

'Our time machine has been completed. Our instruments have detected the enemy time machine in the Sagaro Desert on the planet Aridius. The execution squad has begun.'

Barbara paled. 'Doctor . . . on the screen . . . the TARDIS – here!'

'Even more importantly,' the Doctor added quietly, 'he referred to the TARDIS as the *enemy* time machine.'

The Dalek Prime continued. 'Those who control the TARDIS have interfered with too many of our plans! They are to be destroyed. If necessary, the assassination group will pursue them through all eternity. *Exterminate them*!'

Swiftly, the Doctor turned off the Visualizer, a very worried expression on his face. 'This machine only picks up things that have happened in the past,' he announced grimly. 'Perhaps only a few minutes ago, but the past none the less.'

'Then that means the Daleks are already on their way here,' Barbara whispered in horror.

'Or worse – are already here! They've obviously built a time machine that can follow the TARDIS, and you heard their orders. We are to be exterminated!'

The Doctor, Ian and Barbara had faced – and narrowly defeated – the Daleks twice before. Both times, they had known that there was a possibility that the Daleks might win. The reaches of time and space had always seemed so safe – there was always the chance that if they were being overwhelmed, they could flee. But if the Daleks could now track them down through eternity, then how could they ever feel safe again? Barbara shuddered. 'Can we get away from them?' she asked desperately.

'Yes, yes, yes, I think so,' the Doctor snapped. 'But we must find Chesterton and the child – and we may have very little time! They know nothing of this, and are just having a carefree stroll, remember!'

'The trail just stops,' Vicki observed, in disappointment. Just when things were getting exciting! The sand ahead of them was devoid of further patches of the gooey blood.

'Yes,' Ian agreed. 'And we've come a long way from the ship . . .'

24

Catching the worry in his voice, Vicki nodded. 'I suppose we should start back, Ian. The others'll just be worried about us.'

Bending down, Ian tested the sand with his fingers. It was fine, almost like the kind they used in hour-glasses, he noted. Then his fingers touched something hard, barely an inch below the surface. 'Strange,' he muttered, hunkering down. 'The sand's only a few inches deep. Then there's a rock or something.' Puzzled now, he began to sweep the rock clean. Her earlier resolution forgotten, Vicki joined in helping him, until they had cleaned a patch a couple of feet across.

It was not rock beneath the sand, but glass – or something very like glass. The rays of the twin suns danced off it, but there was no way to see into the depths. Light seemed to fall into it after a few inches. It was like nothing either of them had seen before. Even as Ian watched, the light seemed to be a darkening orange hue. Then he realized that it was no trick of the glass, but the fact that both suns were almost on the horizon. Vicki followed his gaze.

'We really had better go back now.' Vicki started to rise, brushing the sand from her palms on to her dress. She gasped with shock as Ian suddenly clutched her hand and dragged her down again.

'Look at this, Vicki!' he exclaimed in wonder. 'Now the suns are setting, you can see – there's light below this stuff!'

Faintly, in the depths of the glass, Vicki could see what Ian had noticed. There were lights in the material, twisting and moving – or were they *under* the material? Some hidden world below the surface of the sands? Both of them pressed down on to the glass, shielding all stray light from their eyes, trying to get the utmost definition from the lights below.

Behind them, close by the last drop of blood on the trail, the sand began to stir, and then rise. Something rose a few inches, a large trapdoor. There were no lights beneath this, but an impenetrable darkness. Suddenly, from this Stygian cavity, a long tendril lashed out, whipping about Vicki's outstretched foot.

No sooner had it touched than its thick muscles began to contract, drawing its prey back towards the hole. Vicki screamed, twisting to try and see what had caught her. All that was visible was the tentacle, thick, rubbery and oozing that mucous liquid they had mistaken for blood.

At her scream, Ian had twisted around. Veteran of many combats on numerous worlds now, he prepared to defend his companion. Both he and she had forgotten that they were standing now on cleared glass. Neither could catch their footing. Vicki screamed again, struggling to find a handhold to slow her slide into the dark hole, but there was nothing save smooth glass and shifting sands. Ian finally managed to slide forward, reaching to grab her, but before he could do so, a second tentacle whipped from the trapdoor and snared him also. Caught off balance, Ian pitched into the blackness, struggling wildly.

The creature below dragged at Vicki. She tried clutching the edge of the trap, but it had been worn smooth, and her hands simply slid off. With a despairing cry, she followed Ian into the depths.

Slowly, the trap began to close on them.

'Ian! Vicki!' Barbara stood still and called again, cupping her mouth. She listened, but there was no reply. 'Ian!' she called, getting worried now. Surely they couldn't have gone far? It was almost sunset, and they were bound to have started back. She and the Doctor had been walking for almost fifteen minutes now, looking for them. Barbara shivered, drawing the cardigan she had picked up closer about her shoulders. The days were intensely hot, but as in so many deserts, the night promised to plummet below freezing. Already a strong breeze was getting up, caused by the temperature differential.

The Doctor came back into view over the rise, puffing heavily. It was no simple task, walking in the sand, and his silver-capped cane was of little use to help him keep his footing. Before Barbara could ask, he shook his head, and coughed. 'I followed their footprints as far as I could, but then this wretched wind sprang up!' He drew his silk scarf tighter about his neck. 'It's wiped their tracks out completely.' Barbara's eyes glistened, and she wiped them. Pretending that this was because she had sand in them, the Doctor murmured, 'It is blowing up, you know. And getting quite cold.'

'Let's get back to the ship,' Barbara said. 'They might have found their way back by now.' She turned and started back, only to be brought up short by a yell from the Doctor.

'No, no – this way.' He gestured off almost in exactly the opposite direction.

'It was *this* way,' Barbara objected, indicating the way she was going.

Drawing himself fully upright, the Doctor stared haughtily at her. 'You are mistaken, young woman. I have the directional instincts of a homing pigeon. Now come along, and follow me.' He started off on the path he had indicated. Barbara was too dispirited to argue, and followed along behind him. She simply hoped that he did have those instincts he boasted of.

Ian and Vicki had been roughly thrown into a corner of a cavelike opening. The walls were smooth, and close about them. The only exit was straight ahead. As their eyes became accustomed to the gloom, they could both make out some shape blocking that one exit. It was impossible to make much out, but it was large, slimy and had numerous tentacles.

'You all right?' Ian asked, softly. Vicki nodded, massaging the leg where the creature had grabbed her, trying to restore the circulation. Both could hear the wheezing of the creature, as it breathed. It didn't sound too healthy, as if this were not its normal environment. Unfortunately, it was quite strong enough to deal with both of them. Ian tried to move forward. A tentacle lashed out, slamming him back into Vicki, and leaving his chest with a burning welt, even through his blazer.

Clutching his arm, Vicki pointed. 'Look! Down the

27

tunnel – there's more of them!' In the darkness, little could be seen. Yet both could hear a slithering noise, and more of that asthmatic wheezing. 'Dozens of them,' she finished in a tiny, terrified voice.

There was no way for them to tell, but barely twenty feet above their heads, a raging sandstorm was in progress. The wind howled, hurling sand like miniature bullets at the huddled figures of the Doctor and Barbara. She covered her head pitifully with her thin cardigan. The Doctor had tried to spread his coat over them both, clutching it tight to prevent it from blowing away. There was nowhere to hide, nothing to shelter them but each other.

'Cover your mouth and nose,' the Doctor yelled, knowing he would be barely audible over this roaring even a foot away. He gestured for Barbara to take one end of his silk scarf for the purpose. 'It's our only chance!'

Together they tried to stay warm and keep breathing. Sand poured in every crack of their defences, trying to fly into mouth, nose, or their clothing. It was easy to see why the landscape was so featureless if there were storms like this each night! Their only chance was to last through the hours of darkness, and pray that the wind would die when the suns rose again . . .

Light eventually came, and the storm did indeed abate. As light began to penetrate into their makeshift tent, the blasts slowed, and then finally stopped. Hardly daring to believe it, the Doctor and Barbara groaned as they straightened stiffened limbs, then shook their clothing free of the sand that had forced its way into their clothes. Even simply standing upright was sheer agony, as muscles protested, and the sand inside their clothing tore at their skins. Brushing themselves down – and wishing desperately for a bath – they looked around, at first in wonder, and then in mounting horror.

'Doctor,' Barbara exclaimed. 'It's all changed! The whole landscape's changed!' They scanned everywhere, but could see nothing that looked even vaguely like anything that they could recall from the previous night. 'There's no sign of the TARDIS.'

'That sandstorm must have buried it,' the Doctor remarked, bitterly, attempting to shake the sand from his pockets.

In near panic, Barbara gestured wildly about her. 'But where in all of this . . . where *is* it? It all looks alike!'

The two suns had started their climb already. The Doctor estimated that the night had been no more than three hours, and the days promised to be equally short. That meant the suns would reach their zenith in about an hour or so. 'I think we had better start walking,' he suggested softly. 'It's going to be very hot again soon – and we have neither shade nor water.'

Strong as she was, this was getting to be too much for Barbara. They had lost Ian and Vicki, and now the TARDIS. They had suffered through a sandstorm, and were now threatened with heatstroke and thirst. What more could the Universe throw at them?

The Doctor gripped her arm, and hissed, 'Get down!' He followed his own advice.

Barbara dropped, allowing her exhaustion to drag her down. 'What is it?'

'There . . . straight ahead!' the Doctor gestured.

She watched as a small dune began to shake, then to move slightly. Sand began to cascade down, and metal gleamed in the sunshine as a Dalek pushed its way back into the daylight . . .

4

The Victims

The Doctor and Barbara took what shelter they could behind the sands, praying that they had not yet been seen. As they watched, the Dalek finished emerging from the sand, then its eyestick spun about, facing away from them. Two more Daleks moved through the sands to join the first one. One of them, clearly the leader, had instead of the usual sucker-stick, a small instrument like a compass on its arm.

The first Dalek faced the new one. 'The enemy time machine is in this area?'

The leader's eyestick swivelled to see its companion fully. 'Yes. We can locate it with our instruments. Find and destroy it. The remainder will search for the humans.'

'Are they to be taken alive?'

'No. They are to be exterminated.' The Dalek began to move off. 'Destroy on sight! Begin the search.'

The two Daleks chorused, 'I obey!' and moved off in different directions. One came towards the hidden observers, who buried themselves in the sand, trying to remain unseen. The Dalek glided past, and continued onwards.

With a sigh, the Doctor dared a glimpse about. The immediate area seemed clear of their foes. 'We've got to find the TARDIS before they do,' he hissed.

'And we've got to warn Ian and Vicki!' Barbara reminded him. 'They don't even know the Daleks are here!'

The Doctor waved his hand. 'Warn them, yes – but how? It's been hours since we saw them.' Then, realizing that he was depressing Barbara even further, he added: 'However, we'll achieve nothing sitting here. Let's get started.'

They stumbled to their feet, then turned – and froze. Barbara stifled a yelp.

Two strange figures were looking intently at them. Both were almost six feet tall, and thin. Their skins were a deep blue, their heads crested. About their shoulders, they wore long cloaks, of a dark, sandy colour. These were made from the skins of the same creatures that had menaced Ian and Vicki, though the Doctor could not know this. The skins explained how the natives had been seen neither by the Daleks nor by the Doctor and Barbara, for they blended into the sands with perfection.

Barbara glanced at the Doctor, and realized that they were both wondering the same thing: had they escaped the Daleks, only to fall into the hands of another foe?

Ian tried to move gently, without waking Vicki, to bring life back to his deadened leg. It was no use. Vicki woke, startled, and then remembered where they were. She pushed herself away from Ian, who gratefully exercised his cramped leg. They were still in the small cave, and their 'guardian' remained wheezing at the entrance.

'Why are they keeping us here?' Vicki whispered. 'What are they going to do?'

Suppressing the first thought that crossed his mind, Ian hoped that it was nothing more than the product of reading too many stories from that book of monsters in the TARDIS. 'I don't know, Vicki. But you can be sure of one thing . . . we're honoured guests.'

Never one to give up, Vicki asked, 'Can't we do something? How many of them are there?'

'Hard to say.' Ian peered into the gloom, and then was suddenly struck by a realization. 'That's odd – listen.'

Doing so, Vicki said, 'I don't hear anything.'

'Exactly,' Ian answered. 'No wheezing from our captor. No sounds at all in fact.'

Hardly daring to believe it, Vicki peered over his shoulder. 'You . . . you think they've gone away?'

'No, I don't.'

'Then – what?'

Grimly, Ian told her: 'I think that whatever they caught us for is about to start . . .

The Daleks had organized their search well. They had followed the wake of the TARDIS through the Vortex, and knew that they had landed close to the enemy time machine. They spread throughout the sands, looking for any clues. One finally halted, and stared at the sand. There were the distinct impressions of four sets of feet.

'Tracks of the humans,' it reported in.

'Follow them,' came the instructions. A second Dalek came to join the first. 'Perceptors indicate someone is near.'

They looked off, readying their guns. Whoever it was, it must be either one of their enemies, or else a native – in either case, there was only one course of action.

An Aridian came around the side of the dune, saw the two Daleks, and tried to retreat. He had time for barely a step when the combined fire of the two guns cut him down. He screamed, fell, and died. The two Daleks moved forward. The being had fallen in the folds of his long cloak. One Dalek pushed the cloak aside, until they could both see the distinctive blue-tinted skins.

'It is an Aridian,' the first Dalek grated. 'Unimportant. We are continuing our search.'

They moved off, leaving behind them another casual victim of the violence that they carried with them.

At a safe distance, Rynian indicated to the two aliens that it was all right to stop. The Aridians seemed unaffected by the heat even though they were dressed in the thick skins. The Doctor and Barbara were less relaxed. Both sank to the sand with obvious and audible relief. 'The invaders will not find us here for some while,' Rynian noted, in his sing-song voice. 'We may converse freely.'

'Thank you, my dear sir, for your assistance,' the Doctor

32

said, formally. 'This planet is very hard to come to grips with.'

The second Aridian, Malsan, materialized from the dunes. 'This desert was once a vast ocean,' he informed them, sadly. 'We, the Aridians, lived in a magnificent city beneath the seas. Above our dome of glass, exotic fishes swam. Now—' he gestured about himself '—all our world is as you see. Our twin suns burned brighter in the heavens, moving closer to our world.'

'The seas dried up,' Rynian continued for him. 'All the beautiful creatures that lived within their waters perished.'

'All that now live are our people – and the mire beasts,' Malsan added. 'They lived in the slime at the bottom of the oceans. When the waters were gone, they invaded our cities to escape the rays of the burning suns.'

Rynian took up the tale. 'We tried to destroy them, but they multiplied too quickly. We were driven back as the mire beasts took over larger and larger sections of our city.'

The Doctor had forgotten everything else, lost in his fascination of discovery. 'These creatures,' he prompted. 'What do they live on?'

The aliens exchanged glances. Malsan, trying to sound casual, finally admitted: 'They are flesh eaters.'

'Most interesting,' the Doctor exclaimed. 'Now, tell me—'

'Doctor!' Barbara had had enough scientific knowledge for one day. 'We don't have the time for this! Perhaps these people can help us.'

'Mmm? Oh, quite, quite.' He smiled at the two Aridians. 'First things first. Science later.'

'Two friends of ours went out into the desert,' Barbara explained. 'We haven't seen them since. Would you help us find them?'

Rynian inclined his head to one side, thoughtfully. 'When did they set out?'

'Before dark.' Barbara didn't like the glance the aliens exchanged. 'What's wrong? Why do you look like that?'

'The mire beasts hunt at night,' Malsan answered, simply.

'You think your friends are in this area?' Rynian asked.

The Doctor nodded. 'More than likely. I don't imagine

that they would have willingly travelled far.'

Malsan made a peculiar gesture with his hands, evidently of regret. 'Then if the mire beasts *have* taken them, they would have gone through the Taltarian air-lock into the tunnels.'

Suddenly realizing what his companion was getting at, Rynian exclaimed: 'The Taltarian! Then it is already too late.'

'Too late?' Barbara echoed.

Rynian made another gesture. 'Yes. The only way we have discovered of destroying the mire beasts is to entomb them in the sections of the city that they have occupied. To do this, we detonate explosives on the roof of the city, and bury everything beneath.'

Nodding his approval, the Doctor commended: 'An excellent scheme – but what has this to do with our friends?'

The two aliens looked at one another again. Finally, it was Malsan who gave them the bad news. 'The Taltarian air-lock is the next to be destroyed. The explosives are in position, and will be detonated at high suns.'

Barbara stared at them in horror. 'But if Ian's inside . . . We have to stop it!'

Pointing to the sky, Rynian said, 'Already the suns near their peak. We could never reach the air-lock in time.'

Malsan made another of his gestures. 'We shall try. Come.'

The four of them set off across the sands, heading for the doomed air-lock section. Unknown to them, that area was already the scene of feverish activity. A small squad of Aridians was deployed about the entrance to the air-locks. One of them had a palm-sized device, on the surface of which a small light flashed dully in the daylight. From time to time, he glanced up at the suns. The other Aridians, gesturing in their sign language, moved away from the mined area. They had to be well clear by high suns. The mire beasts that they had tracked down were all below in the tunnels, having caught something. One of their fellow citizens was missing; if he were the victim, there was nothing that they could do about it now. He would have to perish, that the race could survive. The best time to trigger the explosives was when the mire beasts were in a feeding frenzy . . .

*

34

Before Aridius had begun to dry up, the mire beasts had hidden in the ooze and mud on the bottom of the seas, waiting for passing prey. Their tentacles had snatched tasty fish, and the beasts had then waited for their next meal. Expending little energy, the creatures needed comparatively little food. Aside from the annual mating periods, they never met with others of their own kind.

When the seas evaporated slowly, the mire beasts had been the only non-sentient life that could adapt. Their lungs, though they worked best in water, could function in the thinner, virtually dry air. Their methods of hunting were unchanged, and they preferred to lie in wait for passing food on the hoof. They had, however, become a community, since there is strength in numbers. Food was far scarcer nowadays, for the tall, intelligent prey that they shared the planet with was far harder to catch. When one mire beast caught anything, it would signal for the community to come and feast, and during the pause it would keep the food live – and fresh. When the other beasts arrived, then feasting could begin.

Ian's surmise that the waiting was over was unfortunately perfectly correct. Through the abandoned Aridian tunnels where they hid from the rays of the suns, the mire beasts moved. They were not quick, and their breathing sounded like rusty hinges. Towards the spot where one of their number had found food, they came. When they arrived, the hunter was ready.

Vicki screamed as a tentacle lashed in, wrapping itself about her. She tried to struggle but the rope-like limb held her tightly in its grip. Before Ian could move, he was likewise a prisoner. Both were roughly dragged from their hole, and raised into the air. In a scene that could have been drawn only in some nightmare, dozens of the mire beasts were gathered about, each waiting for the food to be torn apart and passed about for them all to share. Slavering orifices awaited the small titbits that each would get. Ian felt the pressure increasing, as the mire beast began to squeeze the life out of him.

Above them, the twin suns reached their zenith. In the

sands, the Aridian took a breath, then pressed the lighted button, burying his head into his cloak.

Barely a mile off, two more Aridians paused, and gestured. With sinking hearts, the Doctor and Barbara saw first the position of the suns, and then a huge spray of sand, debris and flame rise into the air. All turned their backs quickly, as the sound, rushing air and heat slapped over them.

Within the air-lock, the effects were even more devastating. The explosives had been perfectly positioned to bring down the roof on the gathered predators. Slabs of razor-sharp glass were blasted deep into the bodies of the creatures. Rock and masonry collapsed upon them. The force of the explosion tore others apart.

Ironically, Ian and Vicki were the only survivors of the blast. Barely out of the small cave where they had been imprisoned during the night, the death of their would-be devourer had sent them spinning back inside. The narrow confines kept any of the shards of glass or masonry from falling on them, and the thick, rubbery mass of the mire beast at the entrance absorbed the effects of the explosion. Aside from bruises all over from hitting the wall, Vicki was terrified but unharmed. As soon as she could, she crawled to Ian, who lay unmoving. Dust and sand made it hard to breathe or see, so she felt instead. His pulse was firm, and she could tell that he was breathing relatively normally. A slight stickiness on the side of his head told her that he had either banged his head, or something from the blast had hit him.

She had no idea what had happened, beyond the fact that they had been literally snatched from the jaws of death. As the noise of the explosion faded away, all she could hear were dying keening noises from a few of the mire beasts. The dust began to settle, and she could see glimpses of daylight through the shattered roof. Between her and safety, however, there was a mountain of rubble and corpses. There was simply no way that she could drag Ian outside again. After a moment's hesitation, she checked his pulse a second time. Still firm. She managed to ease him into a position where he was stretched out.

'I'll get help,' she told him, more to reassure herself than anything, since he was out cold. 'I'll find the Doctor and get help.' Reluctantly, but resolutely, she stood up. Carefully, she began picking her way through the rubble, back the way that the creature had brought them. Now and again, her feet slipped on patches of viscous liquid, or bits of the tentacles. Suppressing the urge to shudder or scream, she worked her way outwards towards the daylight and safety.

Burying their despair in the urgencies of the moment, the Doctor and Barbara allowed the two Aridians to hurry them along. Somehow, the aliens could tell where they were going in this vast wilderness of shifting sands. Eventually, Rynian paused, and began scraping at the sand. The glass-like surface of one of their domes began to show beneath the cleared patch.

'This is one of the old air-locks that we used when our city was beneath the sea,' Malsan explained. 'It will take us to a part of our home that is still free from the mire beasts.'

Nodding his comprehension, the Doctor let the words filter through his consciousness. He was trying to ignore the pain of having almost certainly lost young Vicki and Chesterton. He knew it would be harder for Barbara, and kept the conversation going to give her less time for reflection. 'We appreciate your hospitality, but I must warn you that we are being hunted by a group of evil creatures called Daleks. They would show you no mercy if they discovered that you had given us aid and shelter.'

'We will face that problem when we come to it,' Malsan answered simply. He and Rynian had seen the creatures from the dunes, and both knew that these – Daleks – augured ill for their people. That was one reason why they had agreed to help the Doctor and Barbara. The enemy of my enemy is my friend. 'Meanwhile,' he added practically, 'you need food, water and rest. After that, we shall help you search for your craft.'

Rynian, meanwhile, had uncovered what he had been seeking. There was a small, recessed panel in the glass. Pressing a button resulted in a section of the sand opening

37

to reveal a stairway downwards. 'Please enter,' he invited their guests.

The explosion had disturbed the Daleks briefly, and the Squad Leader had dispatched a Dalek on a flying disc to investigate the area. From its position inside the time machine, the Leader received continual updates. Once the assigned Dalek had radioed back that the explosion had not been an attack, and had merely caused a section of the tunnels to collapse on the predatory beasts of the sands, the Leader gave orders for it to continue the search. As the Dalek did so, it thus moved away from Vicki, who was stumbling through the wreckage . . .

Another patrol called in, and the Leader received their report with satisfaction. 'The seismic detector is registering a contact,' the Dalek informed the Leader. 'The enemy time machine has been buried beneath the sands at this point.'

'Good.' The Leader paused for a moment's thought. 'It must be uncovered before we can destroy it. Take some of the Aridians prisoner and use them to dig the machine out.'

'I obey.'

The Squad Leader regarded the control panel with a good deal of satisfaction. The Doctor and his companions were elusive, but if their ship were destroyed, it could only be a matter of time before the Daleks could track down and kill the human targets. It was time to report to Skaro Base that everything was proceeding as it should.

Soon, their hunt would be over!

5

Deadline

The city beneath the sands was in many ways fascinating. Tall buildings, mostly carved from stone, stretched upwards towards the huge glass domes over the city. The Doctor could imagine how beautiful the view must have been when there was water all about the domes, with sunlight filtering through, the fishes playing . . . Now, all was dark, with the driven sands covering the exterior almost completely. The city had been built with light in mind, and the buildings were now too thickly clustered. Lighting systems had been installed, but these additions had destroyed the architectural sweep of the old city.

Added to that, many of the tunnels to the other domes had been destroyed, to keep the mire beasts out. The Doctor realized sadly that they were present during the last stages of a dying world. There were parks about, supplying the oxygen that the Aridians needed, but they were empty of people. Rynian confirmed the Doctor's guess that the natives now numbered mere thousands. Soon, the Doctor knew – and suspected that they did also – there would be hundreds, then a handful, and then cities empty of all but the ravenous mire beasts. In time, they too would perish from a lack of food. It was sad, but the Universe sometimes cast down an advanced species like this. Probably most of the Aridians clung to life more from habit than from any real desire.

Rynian and Malsan led them to a spacious chamber, and then indicated bowls of vegetables, fruit and water. They then excused themselves, to go and talk with the city elders. Once they were left alone, the Doctor picked up something to eat,

39

and then prowled the room. The natives were friendly, but with the Daleks in the area, it was best to have all of the available exits memorized. The room was of a glossy marble-like material, and contained mosaics and paintings that had long faded with age and had never been renewed. The furniture, too, seemed old, as did the walls. Several of the tunnels that would have led from the room had been filled in with stones and bricks of varying sizes and shapes.

The Doctor returned to the bowls, sampling from them, and offering various items to Barbara. She uniformly shook her head and refused to try them after she had slaked her thirst. 'You should eat,' he said, gently. 'It's really quite excellent, you know.'

Turning a tear-stained face to him, she asked, 'How can you enjoy food when you know Ian and Vicki are . . .' She couldn't say it. Instead, she swallowed, and tried to fight back her tears.

The Doctor put a fatherly arm about her. 'Barbara, my dear, do you really think that I am so callous? No. I feel their loss very deeply, more deeply than I could ever tell you.'

Looking up into his eyes, Barbara could believe him. She tried hard to pull herself together. 'I'm sorry.'

'That's all right.' He patted her shoulder. 'Try and get some rest. I have a strong feeling that in a little while we're going to need all the energy we can muster.'

She accepted his advice. Taking one of the ever-present Aridian cloaks, she folded it into a pillow, and placed it on a raised stone platform. Then she sank down on it. Despite her grief and her fear, the activities of the last few hours had utterly exhausted her. She sank into a fitful sleep almost instantly.

The Doctor nodded to himself, then padded over to the door. He aimed to collar their hosts as soon as they showed themselves . . .

Rynian and Malsan finished their report to the city elders. The First Elder, Prondyn, considered for a moment. 'These strangers admitted that these Daleks sought to kill them, and that they might blame us for sheltering their enemies?'

'Indeed, they were most candid,' Rynian agreed.

A second elder spoke up. 'A patrol reports that one of the scouts was slain by these . . . Daleks. He had no chance, no warning. They appear to be very aggressive. Dare we then defy them for the sake of ones who are not of our kind?'

'They are our guests,' Malsan reminded the meeting.

'They are our *prisoners*,' Prondyn reminded him, gently, 'until such time as the elders decide that they are guests.'

'I am corrected.' Malsan bowed his head.

'My question is unanswered,' the second elder remarked to the meeting at large. Before he could be answered, the entrance door crashed open, and a Dalek moved into the room.

Its gun spun to face the council, and then, slowly and with obvious reluctance, faced down again. Its eyestick centred on the meeting. 'You are the leaders of the Aridians?' it grated.

'We are,' Prondyn said, gravely. 'You have no business here unless invited. You must—'

'Do not attempt to give orders to the Daleks.' The machine-like being moved across the room, examining them. 'You will listen.'

An elder at the far side of the council table rose to his feet. 'We are not barbarians,' he said 'We do not—'

The Dalek raised its gun and fired. In a stench of burning, the elder screamed and died. His body collapsed across the table, but no one dared move to examine it or to protest. 'You will listen,' the Dalek repeated, and all attention was centred on it, and its gun-stick, which significantly had not been lowered. 'The Dalek Leader believes that you have the humans that we seek. You will turn them over to us within one hour, or we shall begin destroying your city. You will also supply us with two natives to clear the sand from our objective.' Its eye swung over them all. 'One hour.'

Turning, the Dalek moved towards the door. Behind it, a babble of voices broke out. Contemptuously, it dismissed the Aridians from its concerns. It knew weakness when it saw it. To save face, the Aridians would talk and debate – but in one hour, they would capitulate and turn over the Doctor and his friends. Such weak creatures as the Aridians were too contemptible even to conquer. Without spirit, they would be poor slaves. Better to kill them all.

The Dalek noted this in its computers. When Aridius was needed, the Daleks would take it. Till then, the natives would be allowed to live – provided they turned over the Doctor and his companions.

The Doctor was eating more of the delicious fruit when Malsan entered the room again. 'I've been looking around a little,' the Doctor said. 'Tell me, why are the openings in the wall here walled up?'

'It led to a part of the city that has been invaded by the mire beasts. There are sections like that all over. We have to block the tunnels to stop their advance. Please sit down. I have news for you.'

From the tone of his voice, the Doctor suspected that it would not be good. He eased himself down on to a wooden bench, and leaned on his cane. 'Very well, what is it?'

After a short hesitation, Malsan admitted: 'The Daleks have contacted us. They have issued an ultimatum.'

'Yes, I suspected that something of the sort might happen.' The Doctor glanced sharply at the alien. 'What is it?'

'We are to hand you and your companion over to them – or they will finish the destruction of our city.'

It was just like the Daleks. 'Yes, yes. I'm afraid they mean what they say, you know. The Daleks don't waste time with idle threats. Have you replied to them?'

'Not yet. The elders of our people are still discussing it. We have a half-sun to give our answer.'

The Doctor shook his head. 'You really don't have any alternative,' he said. 'We certainly don't wish to inflict you with our troubles. We'll leave at once and take our chances.' He started to rise, but Malsan gently pushed him down again.

'No,' he said with regret. 'The Daleks have said that we must hand you over. We cannot do that if we allow you to leave.'

'Then you mean—'

'Yes. You are our prisoners until such time as our arrangements with the Daleks are complete. Then, at the appointed place, you will be handed into their custody.'

The Doctor stared at him with a mixture of annoyance, surprise and sheer contempt. Unable to face the accusing eyes, Malsan retreated. As the Aridian closed the door, the Doctor listened for – and heard – the sound of a bar being lowered.

Their status as prisoners was quite evident.

It had taken a good deal of scrambling for Vicki to reach the surface again. A large section of the tunnels had caved in under the effects of the explosions, and she had been climbing for a while. She heaved herself over the edge of the last bit of rubble – and then dived back down again.

The climb had taken her almost back to the TARDIS, which stood just over the rise from where she now was. That would have been fine – except that there were two Daleks standing by it.

Though she had never personally met the creatures, she knew her history well enough to have recognized them instantly. Added to that, her companions had told her often enough of their past encounters with those terrible foes. She had no idea why they were here, but she was quite certain it spelled serious trouble.

Luckily for her, the Daleks had been concentrating their efforts on seeing that the TARDIS be uncovered. The two Aridians assigned to the task moved away from the battered-looking box.

The first Dalek studied it, then spun its eyestick to face its companion. 'Are the prisoners to go free?'

'No. They are worthless, inferior creatures. They have no value. Destroy them.'

The Aridians began to back away in horror. Both Daleks fired, and the natives crumpled to the sand. Ignoring their victims, the Daleks looked back at the TARDIS. Vicki, peering over the rim, shuddered at the sight.

'Use full power,' the first DALEK intoned. 'Destroy the enemy time machine!'

Both fired again, a long, sustained blast. The TARDIS was bathed in crackling electrical forces, tearing at the structure. Even at her distance, Vicki could smell ozone and the stench of various substances burning off the surface and from the surrounding desert. Then the firing stopped.

The TARDIS was unscathed. Even the paint hadn't been touched.

One of the Daleks moved forward slightly, as if unable to believe this. 'Again!' it snapped. 'Fire!!'

Again, both fired, and again the TARDIS was unaffected.

'It must be constructed of a material that can resist our weapons,' the first Dalek said.

'Remain on guard,' the other replied, 'until the prisoners have been handed over and exterminated.'

'I obey.'

Vicki slipped back quietly into the depths of the tunnel. It was obvious that she could not return to the TARDIS, but it was equally apparent that the Daleks had not yet caught the Doctor or Barbara. There was only one possible thing that she could do – explore the tunnels, and hope that she could find someone native to this world. The Daleks had spoken of prisoners, which had to be the Doctor and Barbara; perhaps, instead of their helping her, she might be able to help them . . .

Barbara awoke with a start, feeling guilty that she had slept at such a time. She sat up, and saw the Doctor sitting, brooding. Reaching out, she touched him and he jumped.

Recovering his calm, he smiled at her. 'Feeling better?'

'Yes.' Barbara was amazed to find that she *did* feel better. The loss of Ian and Vicki was still acute, but she could push it behind her for the moment, coping with what must come. 'What happened while I slept?'

'Nothing very good, I'm afraid.' The Doctor glanced at the door as there came the sound of the bar being withdrawn. Rynian entered the room, somewhat reluctantly. Malsan, looking equally glum, trailed him. The Doctor sniffed. 'This looks like it might be the bad news now.'

'Bad news?' Barbara echoed. 'What bad news?'

'The elders have made their reply to the Daleks,' Rynian announced.

'Well?' the Doctor snapped.

'You are to be handed over when the suns set. The Daleks have promised that when the executions are over, they will leave Aridius – and our people – unharmed.'

Shocked, Barbara realized what he was saying. 'You're going to give us up?'

'What else can they do?' the Doctor asked, being terribly reasonable. 'The Daleks threatened to destroy their city if they didn't.'

'But . . . but . . .' She didn't know what to say. 'Just to be handed over like that . . . Taken out and killed by a Dalek execution squad . . .'

The Doctor shushed her. 'Somehow, some time,' he promised, 'an opportunity will occur. When it does, we must be ready for it. We must grab it as if our lives depended upon it – which, incidentally, they do.'

This hardly reassured Barbara. Ignoring the bearers of bad tidings, she settled back against the wall behind her. Almost unnoticed, a few flakes of mortar fell on to her.

Fighting his way up from the darkness, Ian finally managed to stir. He had had this terrible dream . . . That book he had been reading had come to life. The monster with tentacles had chased after him and Vicki . . . Silly, really. He opened his eyes and sat up, expecting to see his familiar room in the TARDIS.

The blackness remained, and his memory returned. The tunnels, the monsters – both were real. His head hurt, and when he touched the spot, there was blood matted into his hair. He moved forward, and stumbled into the corpse of the mire beast that had caught him. Already, it was beginning to smell. There was no sign of Vicki. On his unsteady feet, he began searching for her.

45

Elsewhere in the tunnels, Vicki made her way cautiously. She was praying that there would be no more monsters, no more tentacles reaching out for her . . . Every step was a nightmare, but she forced herself to continue. Then, from behind her, something clutched her and pulled her backwards. She screamed, but something clamped over her mouth, and stifled her cries. Terrified, she was hauled from her feet, and carried backwards.

Finally, Barbara noticed the small shower of mortar that was dropping on to her. She glanced up, and saw that the trickle was coming from one of the walled-off sections of the tunnels. As she watched, one of the stones moved slightly. She elbowed the Doctor. 'Do you know where this walled-off section leads?' she whispered.

Interrupted in his chain of thought, the Doctor snapped back. 'Mmm? Oh, some other part of the city, I gather. A part that's been invaded.' He sank back into calculating their chances of escape all along the route that they would be forced to take to meet the Daleks.

As Barbara watched, another of the blocked-off tunnels showed signs of life. Again, the stones rocked, and mortar began trickling down. This time, the Doctor noticed it also. Before he and Barbara could confer, the door burst open. In stalked an Aridian, carrying in his arms . . .

'Vicki!'

Barbara jumped to her feet, astounded. Vicki, seeing her companion, kicked out, hitting her captor on the shins. With a howl of pain, the Aridian clutched his leg, releasing her. Vicki ran to Barbara, and hugged her tightly. 'Oh, Barbara, Barbara, Barbara,' she sobbed in relief.

'Vicki . . .' Barbara held her out, drinking in the sheer joy of seeing her. 'We thought that you . . . Ian! What about Ian!'

'Yes, quite,' the Doctor broke in, trying to hide his cracking voice. He had not expected to see the child again, but he had no intention of making a fool of himself by clutching at her. 'Is he alive?'

46

'He got a bad knock on the head,' Vicki answered. 'I made him as comfortable as I could, then came to get help.'

Barbara sighed. 'It might have been better if you had stayed.'

'No, it wouldn't!' Vicki said, excitedly. Now that her visions of being eaten were over, she could start thinking positively again. 'On my way here, I found the way back to the TARDIS!'

'Well, now,' the Doctor said, his eyes sparkling again – *with tears?*, Barbara wondered – 'That puts an entirely different complexion on things. Can you find your way back, do you think?'

With the assurance of youth, Vicki nodded, eagerly. 'Oh yes, I'm sure of it. There was a big iron door, just beyond the entrance over there.'

Barbara allowed herself to hope. Ian alive – and the TARDIS found! 'Maybe we've still got a chance!'

At that moment, Rynian and Malsan entered the room again. Their discomfort was written upon their features, but they were resolved. 'It is time,' Malsan said, sadly. 'I am to take you to the main air-lock.' He reached out to touch Barbara, but she slapped his arm down.

Suddenly, the wall erupted above them. Bricks, stone and mortar showered down on them all. Behind it, a tentacle lashed out, seeking prey. With a scream, both Aridians dashed backwards.

'Sound the alarm!' Malsan howled. 'Mire beast attack in section five! Abandon . . . abandon . . . !'

As the tentacle groped about, the mire beast began to haul itself forwards. Other blocked-off sections showed signs of there being mire beasts behind them. Hidden from the mire beast because they were below it, the Doctor, Barbara and Vicki pressed against the wall, watching the tentacle probe about. With a chuckle, the Doctor gestured towards the door. The panicking Aridians had left an escape route clear!

'Just as I planned!' the Doctor murmured to himself, smugly. He tapped his two companions, and gestured for them to precede him. They dashed for the door, as he covered their escape, brandishing his cane fiercely at the mire beast's tentacle. Luckily for him, the creature was too intent on forcing its way through the opening to attack him. With a final defiant gesture, he ran after his friends.

Following the collapsed tunnel, Ian was actually retracing Vicki's route. Like her, he stumbled after the light. He rose from the tunnel exit, and then prostrated himself swiftly.

The Dalek by the TARDIS glanced in his direction, but decided that there was nothing there but falling stones. It resumed its patrol about the time machine.

Back in hiding again, Ian paused for thought. A Dalek! Here! He hated to think what that meant, but his first course of action was obvious – he had to get it away from the TARDIS, preferably permanently. Struck by an idea, he started hunting around for fragments of the dark native wood he had spotted as he had stumbled through the tunnels . . .

Not far away, Vicki led the Doctor and Barbara back down the route she had been carried by the Aridian. As quietly as they could, they ran for the haven that the TARDIS promised.

The Dalek on guard at the TARDIS spun to face another as it approached. The newcomer halted. 'The prisoners have escaped from the Aridians,' it reported.

'Are we to proceed with the destruction of the underground city?' the guard asked.

'No. Our leader has given them one hour to recapture the humans. If they fail, we shall act.'

'I understand,' the guard acknowledged.

'It is likely that the humans will attempt to return to their time machine. Remain alert.'

'I obey.'

The second Dalek glided away, to join the patrols searching for the Doctor and his companions. The guard Dalek began patrolling once again, alert for any sign of trouble.

★

Ian was working well on his collection of wood. He had almost enough for what he planned when he heard footsteps in the tunnel. Swiftly, he selected the stoutest piece of timber, and waited, silently. To his intense relief, he saw Vicki leading the Doctor and Barbara. He stepped out of hiding, grinning.

Despite Vicki's urgings for silence, Barbara ran forward and grabbed Ian tightly. Ian didn't protest the embrace for a good ten seconds. Then, quietly, he pushed her away.

'What is it, Chesterton?' the Doctor hissed.

'The TARDIS is about twenty yards over the rim, but there's a Dalek on guard.'

Caught in the euphoria of seeing Ian again, Barbara hardly worried about a mere Dalek. 'Then we'll just have to get past him.'

Grinning, Ian showed them his collection of sticks. 'I think I've got a way,' he whispered. 'Barbara, you and Vicki go on up. Be very quiet, and move towards the sand dune to the left.'

The women nodded, and began to move. Ian grabbed Barbara's arm. 'Oh, leave me your cardigan.'

As she slipped it off, Barbara said, 'I'm not going to have any left, the way you use these up!' It seemed as though all of Ian's escape plans tended to use her cardigans. There was that time on Cetus Alpha . . .

'It's not for me,' Ian protested. 'It's for the Dalek.'

'I hope it suits him,' Vicki said, then stifled a fit of giggles. Barbara grabbed her arm, and hauled her up, out of the pit. Ian turned to the Doctor.

'Now it's your turn – let's have your coat.'

'What is this?' the Doctor hissed. 'A plan to defeat the Daleks or to start a jumble sale?

'You'll see in a minute. Stop complaining, and help me with these strips of wood . . .' Ian started to dig them into the sand and rubble by the tunnel entrance. Catching on, the Doctor began helping. After a moment, they had a rough framework set up. Ian spread his blazer and Barbara's cardigan over the frame. The Doctor shucked his coat, and added that. Then they started spreading sand over the rough trap. After a moment, Ian grinned. They both moved back, so that their framework was between them and the Dalek.

'Right,' Ian whispered. 'You go that way, and I'll go this. Find cover, and then we'll take turns . . .'

Ian crawled off about five yards, then hauled himself to his feet. Below him, the Dalek on patrol whirled about, catching sight of the motion. 'Dalek!' Ian yelled, and then dropped back out of sight. 'Oh, dear,' he added, in a loud voice.

The Dalek fired, but its target had vanished. Annoyed, it began to move after Ian. At that moment, the Doctor popped up, said, 'Whoops!' loudly, and then dived for cover. The Dalek's next blast barely missed him. Furious at having missed two targets, the Dalek moved forwards – on to the trap. With a crash, the whole construction gave away, and the Dalek plunged into the tunnel.

Laughing, the Doctor shook Ian's hand. 'Well worth the loss of a coat,' he grinned.

Their triumph was short-lived. Vicki clutched his arm, pointing into the sands. 'More Daleks!'

One of the patrols had been alerted by the destruction of the sentry, and was moving towards the TARDIS. The travellers cut short further congratulations, and ran to the TARDIS. There was an uncomfortable second as the Doctor struggled with the lock. and then they all shot inside the TARDIS. As the doors slammed shut, the Daleks arrived. They began firing at the TARDIS, but with its customary groaning and wheezing, the time machine faded out of normal space.

The Patrol Leader ordered the firing halted. It regarded the traces in the sand, and then said: 'Return to our time machine! We are to follow our enemies wherever they may flee! We shall not be deterred! They are to be found and exterminated!'

6

Flight through Eternity

Within the TARDIS, the mood was considerably different. As they watched the rise and fall of the time rotor in the central console, the travellers laughed and clapped each other on the back, glad to be alive. Vicki, the most boisterous as usual, was hopping up and down. 'We did it! We did it!' she howled.

'Well, of course,' the Doctor said. 'I never doubted for a moment that we would.'

'Oh, come on, Doctor,' Barbara remarked, though not severely. 'You were hardly bubbling over with confidence when the Aridians held us prisoner.'

'Ah, a – momentary qualm, young woman, a momentary qualm. Nothing more.'

'I'll admit I had a few qualms myself,' Ian added. 'Those mire beasts were as nasty as anything we've ever come across.' He picked up the lurid book he had put down several hours earlier. '*This* is going right back into the library, believe you me. I think I'll pick something a little cheerier next time!'

Barbara put an arm around him and hugged him, happy just to have him back from the dead. 'Well, I'm glad those monsters decided to attack the city. If they hadn't . . . Well, I'd rather not think about it.'

Vicki grabbed Barbara's arms, and swung her round, giggling. The euphoria of their escape had quite gone to her head. 'The main thing is we've got away from the Daleks! That's all that really matters.'

Rubbing his hands together in satisfaction, the Doctor beamed at her. 'Yes, I don't think we'll be seeing them again.'

51

Unfortunately, the Doctor had never listened to Plato (assuming that there was precious little that some Greek peasant philosopher could teach a man of *his* accomplishments). The pot-bellied philosopher had squinted at the Doctor, and warned him of *hubris* – the overwhelming pride that makes the gods strike mortals down. Perhaps one day, the Doctor would pay heed to that bit of good advice. No sooner had he spoken than the console began emitting a regular, musical tone, and a small instrument lit up in time with the pulses.

Alarmed, the Doctor began fiddling with the controls, trying to lose that sound and rhythmic light. Nothing that he did had any effect at all. His features fell, and his perpetual frown deepened. All traces of his *bonhomie* had vanished like the seas of Aridius. 'The time-path indicator,' he muttered to himself. 'It's been in the ship ever since I took it, but it's never registered anything before.'

His companions had sobered up, too, realizing that something was wrong. Barbara voiced what they all wondered. 'What does it show?'

'It surveys the time path through which we are travelling,' the Doctor said, rapidly, drumming his fingers on the panel in frustration. 'Both the past and the future. The fact it is registering can only mean one thing . . .'

'Well?' Ian asked. 'Go on.'

Turning to face them, the Doctor announced gravely: 'There's another time machine travelling on the same route that we are taking.

'The Daleks!' Vicki whispered.

'Yes. I'm afraid our celebration was a little premature.'

Ian looked at the flashing light grimly. 'At least we know what we're up against. The Daleks are chasing us through time and space . . .' They all fell silent, as the implications of this began to dawn on them.

Wherever they went now, the Daleks were certain to be just a step behind them . . .

The inside of the Dalek time machine was both similar to

and different from the TARDIS. It, too, was dimensionally transcendental – much larger inside than it looked from the outside. It was smaller than the TARDIS, though, containing two main levels. The instrumentation was all on the ground level, close to the main doorway. Two small laboratories led off from the main control room. Between them, there was an elevator to the upper deck. This housed the taranium power core from which the ship's systems fed. Three Daleks were on permanent duty here, monitoring the highly unstable power levels. Taranium was both the rarest and most unstable element in the Universe. One gram of it could power the time ship for centuries – and it had taken the Daleks two decades to assemble such a large amount of taranium.

By the control panels, the Squad Leader monitored the flight of their ship, and also of the TARDIS, whose path they had locked onto. At the tracking panels, a second Dalek kept them stable on the pathway.

'Compute time lag,' the Leader demanded.

'One five Earth minutes. Reducing.'

Satisfied, the Leader spun to another Dalek behind it. 'We are close. Order the executioners to prepare to disembark. Time to landing – seven minutes.'

'I obey!'

The leader faced the panel again, watching the twin lights moving towards their destination – and the inevitable destruction of their prey!

The inhabitants of the TARDIS were considerably less pleased with the state of affairs. No matter how they tried, none of them could drag their eyes from the flashing light for more than a few seconds. Then, they would look at the Doctor, struggling to override the TARDIS's flight path somehow.

'Useless!' he cried in fury, slamming his hand on the panel. 'Useless!' There had to be a way to do it, but he simply didn't know it, or had forgotten it long, long ago. If only he hadn't lost those notes!'

'No luck,' Barbara sighed, seeing his raging.

'Well,' Ian said, practically, 'if we can't lose them, I suppose we'll have to stop and fight.'

The idea was far from appealing. Vicki looked hopefully at the Doctor. 'We are in front – we could just keep moving.'

'But for how long, Vicki?' Barbara asked, gloomily. 'We can't run forever.'

'And even if we did give them the slip,' Ian added, 'they found us once – presumably they could do it again.'

'Let's ask the Doctor,' Vicki suggested. 'He should know by now one way or the other.'

As they approached him, the Doctor glanced up and shook his head. 'It's no good, I'm afraid. I can't shake them off.'

'Then what happens when we land?' Ian demanded. 'Do we just wait for the Daleks to catch us up?'

The Doctor waved a hand, dismissing the notion. 'It takes our computers about twelve minutes to reorient and gather their power. It is vital that we hold on to that twelve-minute lead until I can find some way of eluding them.'

The idea of running forever didn't appeal to Ian. 'Yes, but—'

The Doctor had had enough. 'Chesterton!' he snapped. 'Leave this to me, will you? Leave this to me!'

Vicki clutched his arm. 'Look, Doctor – the time rotor is slowing down.'

'Mmm?' Cooling off again, the Doctor patted her hand fondly. 'Oh, yes; then in a few minutes, we'll be landing.'

Barbara stared at the rotor, as though willing it to carry on. 'But where, Doctor – *where*?'

Assuming he had a best friend, this hypothetical friend would have been hard pressed to say anything even vaguely complimentary about Morton C. Dill, native of the state of Alabama. At school, he had been unaffectionately nicknamed 'Dill the Pill', a reference to his being rather hard to take. Since his school days – or, as some critics called them, 'school daze' – Dill had not improved. On the contrary, his tendency to spout whatever came off the top of his mind (there being no deeper level to his thinking) was worse than ever. He rarely worried about having any content in his speech. He constantly intruded on others, generally in loud and obnoxious ways. Convinced that he was the life and soul of every party, he would make his way into any gathering and try to take over as quickly as possible.

The general response to his actions was usually a distinct drop in the air temperature, a general move in any direction away from him, and from time to time a proffered fist or a call for the nearest police officer. None of this did much to dampen Dill's enthusiasm; he simply moved on and tried to ingratiate himself into some other gathering, firmly convinced that the original group merely lacked taste. The original group was extremely relieved to merely lack Dill.

It came as a matter of much surprise to anyone unfortunate enough to be acquainted with him that in the summer of 1967, Dill was promptly locked up in a home for the bewildered, where he resides to this day – attempting to drive professionals in the sphere of mental health crazy with his constant, long, rambling discourses. Many of these deal with the event that led to his being incarcerated in the 'joint' (as he insisted on calling the Newman Rehabilitation Clinic) . . .

It had been one of those rare, glorious days in New York City. Fresh in this city – having worn out his welcome in several others – Dill caught sight of the Empire State Building, then the tallest building in the world. Duly paying for a ticket, Dill crammed into the elevator to the observation deck. It was a fast ride, but by the time the car reached the 102nd floor and the doors opened, the rest of the tourists hurried away from him.

The view for once actually kept Dill occupied awhile. As he gazed over the edge of the building, he stared in wonder at the Manhattan streets laid out below him. To the east, Long Island faded into the distance. To the west lay the New Jersey territories, and the Palisades Amusement Park. To the north, the city lay in all of its grandeur. Most notable was the large rectangular of green, Central Park. From his altitude of 1,250 feet, it all seemed so small.

He took the elevator back down to the open-air observation deck on 86th floor, where the pay-binoculars were located, and he could get a better view of the city. Armed with his array of cameras, he knew he'd impress the folks back home with his adventures in the Big Apple. He had very little idea just how unusual those adventures would turn out to be.

He wandered about to the southern side of the building, and the rest of the tourists headed for the other three sides, leaving him alone for a while. He stared out at the Statue of Liberty and the Upper and Lower Bays, then looked about, suddenly realizing that he wanted to talk, and he was alone.

Actually, not quite alone. There was a large, odd-looking blue box that he was certain hadn't been there a moment or two before. Scratching his head, he examined the thing. 'I coulda swore that weren't here just now,' he muttered. 'Well, I guess that's New York for you.'

He was staring at the door handle, working up the courage to open the box, when it opened itself, and an attractive young lady emerged. It was hard to say who was the most surprised, but Barbara was the first to get her wits back. She looked at Dill – dressed in fake cowboy style to 'make a statement' (which most people claimed was 'I have no taste') – and smiled.

'You look like you're from Earth,' she said.

'No, ma'am,' he said, proudly. 'I'm from Alabama.'

'Can you tell me the time?' Barbara asked.

Dill pulled out his genuine gold pocket watch and stared at it. 'About three after twelve, ma'am.'

'No, no, I meant – what *year* is it?'

Dill was aware that this wasn't the normal kind of question even New Yorkers with British accents would ask. 'You have different years here?'

Smiling sweetly, Barbara changed the question. 'What year is it in Alabama, then?'

'1967,' he answered, then slapped his leg and laughed. 'You wouldn't be funnin' me, would you?'

'Oh, no, I assure you.' Barbara was pushed aside, and Vicki poked her head out, staring about her in wonder.

Noticing Dill for the first time, Vicki nodded. ''Morning,' she said brightly.

''Mornin','' Dill answered. Then, glancing at the watch he still held in his hand, '1967.'

'Thank you,' Vicki said, as though it was the most common thing in the world to be greeted with the year. She moved to the rail, and peered about in delight. 'This is ancient New York!'

'*Ancient*?' Dill echoed.

'Oh, yes.' Vicki smiled, happily. 'There were pictures of it in our history books. Mind you, it was mostly destroyed in the Dalek invasion a hundred years from now.'

This was getting to be a little much for Dill. He took off his Stetson, and wiped his forehead. Then he noticed an old white-haired man and a younger man coming out of the box. 'How many more of you folks is in that thing?' he asked.

'Just the four of us, young man,' the Doctor replied.

'Must be a tight squeeze,' Dill remarked. He moved forwards, wondering how four people could fit into such a small box. And a battered one at that . . . How had it gotten here in the first place?

Ian surveyed the cramped confines of the observation deck, then shook his head. 'I don't think this is the place to meet the Daleks,' he said, firmly. 'A lot of innocent people might get hurt.'

'Yes, quite so, quite so.' The Doctor was a trifle annoyed at not having had a chance to say that first. 'The computers will be ready to take us on in a moment. I suggest we re-embark.'

Nodding, Ian called the two females back from their pointing out sights to one another. They headed back for the ship. Dill was still staring in wonder at the little box.

'You goin' back in?' he asked Barbara.

She dragged her eyes back from the horizon with regret. How unfortunate that when the Doctor had returned them to their own time – and only a few thousand miles off course! – they simply couldn't stay. 'Yes,' she said, with real regret. She offered Dill her hand. 'Bye.'

He shook her hand, grinning. 'I saw you all come out, but I doubt seriously you'll all fit back in there – even with your trim figure, ma'am.' As he spoke, all but the Doctor filed back into the box. 'Hey!' he yelped, hit with sudden realization. 'Now I got it! I'll just bet you folks is from Hollywood, makin' a movie! Now that's the truth, ain't it?'

'No, no, that ain't it,' the Doctor snapped. 'Isn't it,' he hastily corrected himself.

Clutching the Doctor firmly around the shoulder, Dill howled secretively into the old man's ear, 'You can tell me – your secret is safe with Morton C. Dill, yessir!'

Forcing his way out of the unwelcome grip, the Doctor repeated blankly: 'Secret?'

'Sure – I seen this trick afore. Great long rows o' folks comin' out of small rooms. It's . . .' he groped for the right words. 'Special effects!'

The only way to evade this idiot seemed to be to humour him. Smiling secretively, the Doctor tapped the side of his nose. 'Special effects, that's right. You just wait, young man – I guarantee you'll see some of the most special effects ever.' He chuckled at his own joke. 'Well, nice to have met you, Mr – ah, Dull, but I have to be going.'

'I knew I was right,' Dill said, pleased at his astuteness. 'You're filming a chase, I'll bet.'

'A chase? Quite right, quite right.' The Doctor popped back into the TARDIS and closed the doors behind him.

'Them movie folks – great sensa humour.' Dill banged on the door. 'Hey, do you know John Wayne?'

With its usual howling, grinding, and complaining, the TARDIS vanished. Dill looked at the space where it had stood, and then shook his head in admiration. 'Now, that's *real* clever special-effects stuff. They're gettin' better at makin' movies all the time.' With his source of interest literally vanished, Dill turned to check the New York skyline and make certain that at least that was still there.

Behind his back, and far quieter than the TARDIS, the Dalek time machine materialized. After a few seconds, Dill turned round, and almost jumped out of his neatly pressed cowboy suit. 'Goddarn it, they've done it agin!' he exclaimed, with a whoop. 'Them movie folks!'

The door to the box opened, and a Dalek emerged, looking about for any signs of the TARDIS. What he saw instead was a remarkably foolish-seeming human, laughing. The Dalek scanned the figure, and realized that it was dressed in period clothing, so was definitely not one of the TARDIS travellers.

Dill slapped the Dalek hard on the casing. 'Howdy, mister,' he laughed, tears streaming down his face. 'Well, you sure are an ugly-looking critter!' he peered into the Dalek's gun, then tried to shake it by the arm. Annoyed, the Dalek moved its arm, throwing the idiotic human aside. Offended, Dill scowled at the Dalek. 'Well, there ain't no need to act sore. Those other movie folks was downright hospitable.'

'Where are they?' the Dalek grated. Perhaps this maniac would serve some function after all.

'They just . . . left,' Dill explained. 'They was in some beat-up old blue box. It just . . . sorta . . . well . . .vanished.'

The Dalek stared at Dill. For a brief second, his life was almost over; then the Dalek disarmed its gun. It was far worse for the human race to allow this fool to live on. Turning, the Dalek re-entered the time machine.

Readying his camera, Dill looked up in annoyance. 'Hey, mister,' he howled. 'Hold on there! I'd like to get a picture with you an' me in—'

The time machine vanished.

Lowering his camera, Dill muttered, 'Darned if they didn't do it agin!' He moved forward, and started examining the area where both boxes had stood. There had to be a trick to it, and he'd find it out. No one could fool Morton C. Dill! He went on his hands and knees tapping at the structure, and calling out for the pretty lady or ugly critter, without any luck at all.

At that moment, two of the tower guards came around the corner of the building. They watched Dill's feverish search, and yells for what seemed to be tiny folk living inside the bricks. After a moment, the senior guard turned to his companion.

'Keep an eye on him, Sal. I'm gonna get a cop. Make sure he don't try to jump, or nothin'. He looks loony enough to try anything.'

Naturally enough, when the cop arrived, Dill attempted to explain everything. It did get him a sympathetic hearing for the first time in his life – and a one-way ticket to the Sanitarium.

Within the TARDIS, the mood was grim. All four travellers clustered about the time path indicator. It was still registering strongly.

'They're still after us,' Ian observed, rather unnecessarily.

'Yes,' the Doctor agreed, morosely. 'And I'm afraid the gap is closing. Their time computers must work faster than mine.'

'Does that mean they'll catch up?' Vicki asked.

'Well, if we can't shake them off, of course they will, child!' the Doctor snapped. His nerves were worn from the frustration of failing to lose their pursuers. 'Every time we make a landing, the Daleks draw closer.'

'Then sooner or later we're going to *have* to face them,' Barbara pointed out.

'I'm afraid so.'

Action was what Ian wanted; running away never solved anything, to his mind. 'The best we can hope for is that we meet them in a planet with the right sort of conditions where we can put up a fight.'

'Quite so, quite so,' the Doctor agreed. Though he had spent many years on the move through space and time, he also realized that the Daleks would never rest until they had found his track again. The issue had to be resolved, one way or the other. Either he would win, or the Daleks would.

Vicki was staring at the controls, willing what she had seen to be wrong. When it persisted, she said in a nervous voice: 'We're landing again, Doctor.'

'Already?' Barbara asked, appalled.

'Yes, already,' the Doctor snapped, moving around to his instruments. 'Our only chance now is to find a place to meet and defeat the Daleks!'

Curiously enough, the people that they were about to meet had also set out from New York – but 95 years earlier, on Tuesday, 5 November, 1872 . . .

60

7

Nightmare

The breeze was stiffening in the sails, the deck creaking beneath his feet. The waves crashed against the brigantine's bows as she ploughed through steady seas, a sound First Mate Albert G. Richardson loved. The smell of the spray, the feel of a good ship beneath his feet, the pathways over the deep – at twenty-eight, he was more than contented with his life. Raising the telescope to his eye, he could make out the blurred smudge that indicated land on the horizon.

'Land about six miles off, to Sou' Sou'-West,' he reported.

Captain Benjamin Briggs, master and part-owner of the brigantine, glanced up. He was a stern-featured New Englander of thirty-seven, and a devout Christian. He was also the best captain that Richardson had sailed with, firm and strict, but also with a gentleness that prevented his being tyrannical. 'Aye, that'll be the island of Santa Maria,' he commented, fingering their position on the chart. 'We're making good time, Mr Richardson. If the wind holds, we shall reach Genoa a good two days ahead of time.'

Richardson nodded, equally pleased. They had had some rough weather, but nothing that they couldn't handle with ease. The ship was a delight, and barely half-laden – just 1,700 barrels of alcohol in the extensive hold. That was enough to turn a profit in Italy, and not so much as to make the ship wallow. 'I'll mark the reading in the deck log.'

He crossed to the slate board, glancing at the ship's chronometer as he did so. Then he wrote, in his neat, precise hand: 'At 8 eastern point bore S.S.W. 6 miles distant.' That would serve until the entry could be transferred to the ship's log as the first entry for 25 November.

'I'm going aft, if you should want me,' Briggs said, leaving. It was his custom to spend a part of the morning with his wife, Sarah, and their two-year old daughter, Sophia Matilda. Richardson smiled. The child was a delight to all of the sailors aboard, and Mrs Richardson was always ready with a kind and encouraging word.

Alone, Richardson held the wheel loosely, and looked out to sea. He could hear the noises from the galley, where the cook-cum-steward, Edward William Head, was finishing putting away the dishes after breakfast. Head firmly believed in keeping his galley tidy, and would not be seen until everything was put into its correct place. Second Mate Andrew Gillings would be bunked out now, getting his rest after a night at the wheel.

The four sailors – German-born, but American citizens now – were down in the holds, checking the alcohol barrels. All of them knew that in confined spaces, those wooden barrels might leak, and alcohol fumes could build up. Ships had been known to have their hatches blasted open and fires begun due to such fumes. Accordingly, the first task for the men each morning was to check to ensure that this was not so. Though the ship had three hatches – fore, middle and lazarette in the after section – the ship's boat was lashed to the middle hatch, so it couldn't be opened unless the boat was moved. Accordingly the men – Arien Martens, Gottlieb Gottschalk and the two Lorenzen brothers, Boy and the older Volkert, had opened the fore and lazarette hatches and aired out the hold.

As he was listening, Richardson heard a strange noise from the lower deck – a sound that in all his years of sailing no ship had ever made. It seemed like a crashing noise of timbers, metals and glass, rhythmically sounding. As he was getting worried, the noise ceased. Perhaps it had been some noise carried over the surface of the sea?

It was, in fact, the arrival of the TARDIS. It had materialized below the deck house, out of his line of sight. After a moment, Barbara stepped out. 'It's a ship all right,' she called back over her shoulder. 'A sailing ship, at sea.'

Moving up to join her, Ian glanced about. There was no one in sight, and the place looked and sounded peaceful. 'Don't wander away, Barbara. Please.'

Barbara stepped out of the TARDIS, peering about. 'I'm just looking,' she said, defensively.

'There's no point in being seen,' Ian objected.

'If they don't see me, they'll see the TARDIS.' She gestured at the empty deck. 'Anyway, we can't come to much harm here, can we?'

'We'll only be here a few minutes,' Ian said, sensing that he was losing this argument. 'The Doctor's resetting the controls now.'

Nodding, Barbara took another couple of tentative steps. She had never been on a ship like this before, and the swaying of the deck was almost restful, in an odd way. She just wanted to gaze out over the open seas. Walking carefully to the rail, she stared out at the miles and miles of ocean. The scent was pure and clean, the air tangy with salt. She breathed deeply, enjoying the moment for as long as it could last.

It wasn't long. Richardson had seen a figure on deck, and first assumed it to be one of the crew, come up to report. With a shock, he realized that it was a *woman*, in slacks and a shirt! Startled, he opened the cabin door quietly, and moved up behind her, then lunged. 'Got you!' he exclaimed.

Struggling, Barbara tried unsuccessfully to break free. 'Let go of me!' she cried.

'Oh, no you don't!' Richardson said with a laugh. 'Captain Briggs will want to meet a stowaway.'

'I'm *not* a stowaway,' Barbara snapped. 'Take your hands off me!'

Richardson got a firm grip on both her wrists, then stood, panting, and looking her over curiously. Apart from her peculiar clothes, her hair was styled strangely, and she wore very odd shoes. 'Where have you been hiding since we set sail?' he asked. There wasn't much room aboard, and Head had not complained of any missing food. This was a peculiar matter. Nor did she sound American, but rather English.

'Please,' Barbara begged, 'you're hurting my hands. And I haven't been hiding. I've only just arrived.'

63

Richardson laughed at that. 'Right you are! I'll bet you're a mermaid, fresh lost her tail, and just arrived on board after spying our ship from Santa Maria there, right? Feeling sorry for us poor, lonely sailormen, I'll warrant!'

'If I told you the truth,' Barbara answered, 'you simply wouldn't believe me.'

'I believe what I *see*,' the mate answered, significantly. 'Now come on – you're going afore the Captain.'

Despite her struggles, Richardson managed to drag Barbara forwards. What he didn't see was Vicki, peering around the cabin door. She had followed Barbara out for a breath of sea air, and stumbled across the problem. Glancing about, she saw a rack of belaying pins. Carefully, she picked one up, then hefted it. It should just about do the trick . . .

Within the TARDIS, the Doctor straightened up, finally. 'There we are,' he announced. 'Everything in order.'

'Good.' Ian looked at the picture on the scanner screen. It showed the side of the ship, and the sea beyond. 'I don't think a sailing ship is the best place to fight the Daleks. It's too confined.'

'Indeed. Anyway, we're ready to move on.' The Doctor waved a hand at the door. 'Perhaps you'd be good enough to call the ladies, um?'

'Yes. The quicker we get away from here, the better.'

Richardson was dragging Barbara across by the cabin when everything went black for him, and he pitched down on to the deck. Surprised at this, Barbara glanced up, and saw a grinning Vicki perched on the ladder to the upper deck. In her hand, she held the belaying pin.

'Well done, Vicki,' Barbara said, with relief. 'Thanks.'

Giving a half-bow, Vicki laughed. 'Delighted. Any time.'

Both heard the next set of footsteps at the same time. 'There's someone else!' Barbara whispered in alarm. Vicki shot back under cover, and Barbara hid behind the cabin door. With relief, when the person appeared, Barbara saw that it was Ian. Before she could say anything, though, Vicki sprang out and hit down with the pin.

'I got him! I got him!' she exclaimed, excitedly. Then she saw who she had hit, and was instantly contrite. Dropping the belaying pin, she jumped down.

Barbara stooped to help Ian to his feet. The pin had caught him a glancing blow, so he was stunned rather than unconscious. 'Help me get him inside the TARDIS,' Barbara said to Vicki, who scurried across to help support Ian's weight.

'Oh, Ian,' she said, 'I'm terribly sorry. Did it hurt?'

Barbara snorted, as she struggled to drag him across the deck. 'That's a silly question.'

'I didn't mean it,' Vicki moaned. 'Oh dear!'

'Hold him up,' Barbara warned, and together they managed to manoeuvre him back into the TARDIS.

There was a groan on the deck, as Richardson struggled uncertainly to his feet. Vicki's blow had merely stunned him too, but his head felt like it was splitting. He had seen what looked like three figures heading across the deck. Staggering to the edge of the cabin, he was astonished to see a large blue box on the mid-deck. Then, a second later, he was just as astonished *not* to see it.

Somehow, it had vanished.

That blow on the head had done more damage than he had thought! Shaking his head to try and clear it, he yelled, 'Captain! Captain! Captain Briggs! Amidships!'

The Lorenzen brothers popped their heads out of the for'ard hatchway, wondering what was happening. The Captain hurried on deck himself. 'What is it, man?'

Rubbing the back of his neck, Richardson tried to straighten up. 'Captain,' he explained, 'I found a stowaway, sir. A girl, it was. She . . . she managed to get away from me.'

'Stowaway, eh?' Briggs muttered. 'A girl, you say?'

'Aye, sir.'

Firmly, Briggs nodded. 'All hands amidships,' he called to the brothers, who nodded, and called below in their turn. Turning back to Richardson, he continued. 'How did she get away?'

'I got hit over the head,' his mate explained, fingering the swelling lump that was there.

'By her?'

'No,' Richardson said slowly. 'Come to think of it, it couldn't have been. I was holding her in front of me. I *think* I saw two more people with her . . . but I was pretty much out of it, sir.'

'Then it would seem that we have more than one stowaway aboard.' He glanced up as the four sailors, the cook and a yawning second mate appeared. Martens looked worried, having caught the last part of this conversation.

'I don't like it, Captain,' he said. 'We've been about the ship too much for there to be room for a single person to hide out – let alone two. Maybe they wasn't *people* . . .' He crossed himself, fervently. 'Maybe they was Krakens, or mermaids.'

Briggs looked at him in pity. 'This is *Eighteen Seventy-Two*, sailor,' he snapped, 'not the Dark Ages! Mythical creatures do not exist. If there's a woman aboard, it's a woman and nothing more. Now, we're going to search the ship and do a thorough job of it.'

The sailors didn't believe that it was possible for them to have missed seeing a single stowaway, let alone the two or three that the First Mate claimed were about. Still, orders were orders, so they set to with as much enthusiasm as they could muster for the task. As always, the two Lorenzen brothers worked as a team. They headed for'ard, and looked everywhere that they could think of on deck. They found – as they had expected – nothing.

'May as well try below,' Volkert muttered, and turned to go back. He froze in horror.

Approaching him was some *thing* made of metal. It had no apparent source of motion, yet it was gliding across the decks towards him and Boy. Volkert managed to get his arm functioning enough to tap his brother on the shoulder. Boy turned, then likewise froze, regarding this impossibility with dread.

'Where are the time travellers?' the Dalek grated. It had

just emerged from its time machine, and could not see any sign of the TARDIS.

'Gods of the deep!' Volkert cursed. How could such things come aboard unless they were spirits? Nothing could induce him to stay on a haunted ship! He regained his power to move, and shot past the creature, not even pausing to see if his brother was following. He skidded to a halt by the cabin, as another of the creatures emerged from a shining box on the mid-deck. Martens ran across to join Volkert.

'It's the folk of the sea!' he howled, in fear. 'They've come to drag us down! We can't stay on this cursed ship!'

Volkert had worked that out already. He began scrabbling at the fastenings that held the ship's boat lashed to the mid-hatch. Martens helped him, working as fast as they could. The boat began to lurch free, but not soon enough. One of the creatures had spotted them, and glided across to the two sailors.

'Stay where you are!' it ordered. 'You will provide information. Where are the time travellers?'

This was too much for Volkert. Without waiting for the boat, he screamed, jumped to the rails and then leapt into the sea. As Martens rushed to join him, the Dalek fired. For a second, Martens hung on the ropes, screaming in agony, then his dead body twisted and fell into the sea.

His screams had alerted the rest of the crew. Mrs Briggs, fearing some terrible shipwreck, ran onto deck, holding a wailing Sophia Matilda. As the Daleks began to search the ship, the other sailors panicked, and dived overboard to escape these infernal beings.

Briggs and Richardson tried to finish launching the ship's lifeboat. Mrs Briggs stood, pale-faced and terrified, by the rail. One of the Daleks saw them, and moved forward. Knowing how fast the humans could dive into the water, the Dalek moved too rapidly itself, trying to prevent their escape. Instead, as their ship rolled slightly, it crashed into the woman and child.

Mrs Briggs screamed once as she fell. The Dalek keeled forward, dropping after her. The three of them hit the water together, but only the mother and child resurfaced. The

Dalek, weighed down by all of its metal, sank swiftly from sight.

Richardson abandoned his efforts with the lifeboat, now almost free, and ran with Briggs to glance over the side of the ship. Sarah Briggs was desperately trying to reach her daughter. Briggs dived into the water to help. Richardson hesitated for a second. The ship rolled again, and the lifeboat, now completely unlashed, slid across the deck and slammed into the Mate's legs. Richardson fell over the side, swiftly followed by the boat, still upside-down, as it had been stored. It hit the water, rolled, and sank.

As the sailors, Sarah Briggs and the child tried to stay afloat, they saw their ship moving swiftly away from them. It would only be a matter of time before they followed that evil creature down to the depths. They were better than seven miles from land, and there was no chance that any of them could swim that far . . .

On the ship, the Daleks were totally uninterested. They completed their search, and then reported back to their squad leader. 'There is no one on the vessel.'

'Then our enemies have escaped us again. We will continue the pursuit.' It led the way back into the time machine. After a moment, the metal box vanished, leaving the decks completely clear.

The wind was full, and the sails caught the breezes. The ship moved on, with no hand on the wheel. The decks creaked, the sails filled, the wheel spun. It would be found on 4 December, floating like this, by a sister ship, the *Dei Gratia*. The *Dei Gratia* had left New York eight days behind this vessel. They had been in the same dock area. Their captains had taken dinner together. They would never do so again. Midway between the Azores and Portugal, the *Mary Celeste* was sighted, and then boarded.

No one was aboard. The mystery had begun.

Within the TARDIS, Ian had just about recovered, and was suffering Barbara's ministrations. She had bathed the lump on his skull, which was already starting to subside. 'That better?' she asked.

'Somewhat,' Ian agreed. 'Did you see the name of that ship?'

Barbara nodded. 'The *Mary Celeste*,' she answered, troubled. 'Ian, you know what must have happened after we left, don't you?' I mean, we all know that the *Mary Celeste* was found abandoned, her crew vanished. The Daleks must have gotten them somehow.'

'I don't know.' Ian looked at her, gently. 'That must be the answer to the mystery. But it's an answer no one would believe.'

'That's not what worries me.' She began to tidy up the medical supplies, returning them to their cabinets in the tiny infirmary that the TARDIS possessed. She was working just to keep occupied, while she tried to quell her troubled heart. 'Ian, whichever way I look at it, I can't help feeling that *we* killed those people. If we hadn't landed there, the Daleks would never have found them and killed them. It's our fault.'

Ian shook his head, firmly. It hurt, and he tried to fight down the pain. 'It isn't, you know. But – well, we learned about the *Mary Celeste* when we were just children. It is a fact of history, Barbara. One thing we should have learned in all our years of travelling is that, whatever we do, we can't change history.' He smiled at her, tenderly. 'You tried that with the Aztecs, and failed.'

'I know.' Barbara managed a feeble smile. 'Yet it doesn't help me much. Maybe you're right, and maybe it was inevitable that those poor sailors had to die. I still can't help feeling that it's still partly our fault. We led the Daleks there, you know.'

'All right,' Ian suggested. 'Think about this. Suppose we had never travelled with the Doctor. Suppose he alone had landed on the *Mary Celeste*, unaware of what she was. Would it then have been his fault?'

'Well . . .' Barbara began to weaken. 'I don't think so. It would have been an accident.'

'Then why is it our fault? Just because we happened to know what the ship was?'

Barbara tried to express what she was feeling. 'We . . . well, we *did* know. And we did nothing.'

'And what could we do?' Ian asked reasonably. 'Should we have told the crew that there were Daleks arriving any minute, and invited them into the TARDIS? Do you seriously think that they would have come?'

The idea was rather ludicrous. 'They'd probably have made us walk the plank.'

Ian stood up and put a hand on her shoulder. 'I think that there was nothing that we could really have done. In one sense, yes, it was our fault that the Daleks found the ship. On the other hand, we know that if they hadn't, then something would still have had to happen to kill the crew. They were fated to die, I'm afraid.' He sighed. 'Come on, let's see how the Doctor's doing.'

They returned to the main control room, where the Doctor was still struggling with his instrumentation.

'Any change, Doctor?' Barbara asked, not really expecting any news.

'I've altered the time curve we were following,' the Doctor said, without enthusiasm. It had taken all of his ingenuity to manage that without his manuals and notes. 'For a moment, I dared hope that we had lost them – then they must have detected the change and altered their own course again. They're still right behind us.'

The way he said this worried Barbara. 'We still have our twelve-minute lead, surely?'

The Doctor shook his head. 'I'm afraid that's down to eight minutes now . . . and it'll be reduced even further after our next landing. The Daleks are catching up with us.'

All four of them turned to look at the path indicator. It seemed to pulse brighter and bleep louder – the signal of impending doom . . .

8

Journey into Terror

It was not a place to be comfortable. The hallway was huge, made of stones and mortar dating back to the seventeenth century. It had lasted three hundred years or more without obvious change, and would last the same again with ease. Grey stones of immense size and strength laid out the large foyer. In the background stood a staircase of immense size. Each step was almost ten feet wide, and all were carved from a solid block of granite. This led to upper storeys that were deeply shadowed.

The hall and foyer themselves were shrouded in gloom. Pictures, faded and covered in dust and cobwebs, had long since given up trying to brighten the place. Now, they were content to hide in the darkness and hope to be overlooked. Large windows, filled with expensive stained-glass decorations, probably hadn't been cleaned for centuries. Outside, lightning flashed, but even that could make little impact on the blackness within. The crash of thunder echoed about the empty rooms.

Nothing moved – no rodents, no insects. The shadows alone seemed to creep about, scurrying from patch to patch of blackness. Yet, even without any signs of life, there was something eerie about the whole place. It was more than the mystique that old things possess. It was as if there were some brooding evil that had, centuries past, settled into those cold stones and somehow animated them.

It was not a place to be comfortable.

If there were any strangers bold enough to cross the oaken threshold, they would peer about, sensing eyes in the gloom, eyes that watched and hungered – desiring the vitality of the still-living to feed their dead, yet undying, needs. Even where nothing lived, there was still that terrible sense of intelligence – watching, patiently, for its prey . . .

The TARDIS materialized near the door. For a moment, the light atop the time machine cast fresh, clean rays across the aeons of dust. Then the light cut out, and the darkness settled back down to wait again. After a moment, the door of the TARDIS opened, and – first as ever – Barbara peered out.

She looked at the hallway, and shuddered. 'I'm not wild about this place,' she muttered. It felt like a tomb. *Her* tomb.

As she moved out, her three companions followed. Ian glanced about, examining the place from a tactical point of view. 'I don't know,' he commented. 'It might be an ideal spot to wait for the Daleks.' He slapped a stone. 'Thick, stout walls.' He gestured up the stairs. 'An upper storey. The Daleks aren't too good on stairs, don't forget.' He moved over to the staircase, to check that the steps were still navigable. He rested his hand on the carved wooden handrail as he did so.

Instantly, there was the sound of fluttering, as something came to life in the huge, arched rafters of the room. Vicki gave a squeal, and they all tried to peer through the gloom to see what was making the noise. Whatever it was, it was getting louder. Outside, another jagged fork of lightning split the sky. The little illumination it provided helped the travellers to see just dimly. Hundreds of furry shapes, with outstretched wings and fanged faces . . . Eyes gleamed redly in the light. As the lightning faded, the thunder crashed, drowning for a second only the beating of hundreds of tiny wings.

'Bats!' Barbara shuddered. 'They're bats!'

The wings beat on, as the bats flocked out. One of the windows over the stairs had a section missing near the top. The four friends could see the cloud-like mass of bats fluttering through this opening, and then they were gone.

Vicki opened her eyes again, and looked about the room. 'Probably vampire bats,' she said, in a hollow voice.

Ian glanced down at her, and raised an eyebrow. 'Charming.'

'Nonsense!' the Doctor snorted. 'Vampire bats are only to be found in South America.'

Vicki moved closer to him, and he put an arm about her, protectively. 'Perhaps that's where we are?' she suggested, with a shudder.

'Mmm . . . I doubt it.' The Doctor gestured at the walls with his cane. 'Judging by the style of architecture, it's more likely to be Central Europe.'

'Well, wherever we are,' Ian said firmly, 'I'm with Barbara. I don't like it here. I think we should go.'

'In normal circumstances, I would agree with you,' the Doctor answered. 'But with the Daleks to face, it's essential that we have a look around. Come along, Chesterton – let's see what's upstairs.'

That was definitely too much for Barbara. 'Well, you can go if you want to, but I'm staying right here.'

'Me too,' Vicki added. The closer she was to the TARDIS, the safer she felt. She couldn't shake the feeling that they were being observed. The Doctor evidently didn't share this impression.

'Very well, very well,' he agreed. 'We won't be long.' He gestured to Ian, who nodded, and they walked off up the stairs.

Watching them leave, Vicki and Barbara drew closer to one another, both seeking reassurance. Glancing down at Vicki's ashen face, Barbara realized that the young girl was really frightened. Coming from so far in the future, she'd probably never been in a stately home even. Poor thing, and here she was – a grown woman – acting like a nervous child. It was up to her to set an example.

'You know, Vicki,' she said, with a bravery she didn't really feel, 'there really isn't anything to be scared about. I mean, it's just an old house. We're letting our imaginations run away with us.'

Even as she spoke, there was another blast of lightning, and tremendous crash of thunder. Without thinking, they clutched one another in panic. Then, ashamed, they released their grip again.

'We've got to stop this,' Barbara said, firmly. 'We're just being silly. We need something to occupy our minds. Let's help the Doctor, and look around for anything that might help us fight the Daleks down here.'

Though none too enthusiastic about the idea, Vicki nodded. She made sure, however, that she stayed close to Barbara when they began their search of the room. This was one time when she had no intentions at all of striking out alone!

Close by the TARDIS was a shadowed niche. In it was a large wooden chest, amply covered with dust and cobwebs. This was about six feet long, and three feet high and deep. Barbara brushed at the cobwebs, uncovering deeply carved reliefs in the dark wood. Vicki shuddered, as most of the carvings depicted scenes of torture.

'I wonder what's in it?' she said, not sounding as if she cared at all. 'Someone has horrible taste in home decor.'

'It's probably empty,' Barbara replied, 'but we can't pass up anything so obvious, can we?' She reached out to try and open the lid, then hesitated. Maybe she was wrong; in a house like this, there could be almost anything inside. As if to echo her gloomy fears, there came another blast of lightning, and a deep-throated rumble of thunder. Determined, Barbara tried to lift the lid. It was heavier than she thought, and she had to apply both arms and a good deal of straining to move it at all.

Naturally, it creaked terribly as it swung open. Inside, there was a gleam of white in the low light and, with a shudder, Barbara realized that she had opened a coffin. A skeleton lay within, partially clad in decayed garments. Even as she was repulsed, one of the bony arms jerked.

The thing sat up slightly, turned its head and then the jaw fell open. Peals of demonic laughter echoed about the room. With a shriek, Barbara let the lid drop down. Clutching Vicki, Barbara retreated back to the TARDIS. Both of them kept their eyes firmly fixed on the coffin, waiting to see if the spectre would follow.

Things were a trifle calmer at that moment for the Doctor

74

and Ian. They had climbed the stairs and, after an obligatory rest for the Doctor to get his wind back, moved on down the corridor towards a set of double doors. The dark walls were lined with more paintings, draperies, and several suits of armour, all needing a good polish to restore them to showcase quality.

As the two figures passed by, several helmets swivelled to follow their progress. Ian paused to grimace at one particularly macabre painting. From the draperies behind him, a thin gauze-wrapped arm groped outwards towards his neck. Without even noticing, Ian continued after the Doctor. The arm wavered for a second or two more, then withdrew.

In his usual direct fashion, the Doctor had marched to the large doors, and then thrown them open. Inside the room was a jumble of very odd equipment. In the centre of the stone floor was a table on some kind of support that could be raised and lowered. Chains from the table led to a capstan in one wall. The Doctor's eye followed the path the table would take, seeing a huge skylight in the roof. Lightning traced a crooked path across the small patch of black sky.

About the walls were huge coils, switches the size of a man, and what appeared to be large vacuum tubes. One wall held a bank of panels, clearly marked in English indicating voltage, amperage and wattage. These measured thousands of each unit, which struck the Doctor as being more than a trifle unrealistic.

Ignoring this for a moment, the Doctor moved forward to examine the table. It was covered with a grey sheet that had probably once been white. Wiring ran from the equipment across the floor and disappeared under the sheeting. It seemed connected to what looked uncomfortably like a large, thick-set body. It all rang a familiar chime in the back of the Doctor's mind, but he couldn't quite place it.

A tap on his shoulder made him start, but it was merely Ian. 'Kindly don't startle me when I'm concentrating,' the Doctor snapped.

Grinning in disbelief, Ian answered: 'Concentrating? Right. So, what have you found now?'

'Well, it's obviously some kind of laboratory, Chesterton,

the Doctor retorted, annoyed at having appeared frightened. 'Look at this equipment.'

'Yes,' Ian agreed, looking around. There was something awfully familiar about this place, but he couldn't quite put his finger on it. 'Well, I think we've discovered one thing – this is no place to meet the Daleks. Let's find Barbara and Vicki and get out of here.'

'Not until I've seen what's on that table,' the Doctor answered, firmly.

Eyeing the shrouded shape, Ian put a hand on the Doctor's shoulder. 'I'd be happier *not* knowing, Doctor.'

Surprised, the Doctor looked up at him. 'You can't mean that, my boy,' he remarked. 'Where's your sense of adventure, your scientific spirit?'

'It died a slow and painful death when we were buzzed by those bats.'

Snorting, the Doctor broke Ian's grip. 'Well, stay here then while I look.' He set off towards the table. As he passed the first of the huge tubes, they sprang into sudden life. With a hum, rings of incandescent light began to pulse upwards through the glass.

Retreating to rejoin Ian, the Doctor stared raptly at the phenomenon. The rings of light rose in stately motion to the tops of the tubes, where they vanished. The panels of instruments began registering as fresh bands of light began their journey up the tubes. These rings were moving faster, and the hum from the machinery became louder. The crash of the thunder overhead was almost drowned out.

Suddenly, two large globes on armatures swung from the panels, until they were over the shrouded table. As the light display intensified to nearly painful brilliance, jagged arcs of electricity passed between the globes, enveloping the figure on the slab. Then the room went dark.

It took a moment for their eyes to readjust to the gloom. As they did so, Ian saw that the shape on the table was starting to move. An arm reached upwards, and then the rest of the figure followed it. The cloth covering fell free, and Ian and the Doctor were staring at a horrible apparition.

The creature was made from sewn-together pieces of

cadavers. The stitching was still visible, and not at all pretty. It had little hair, a squared head, and twin bolts in its neck. Its clothes were ragged and dark. Twin red eyes burned under huge brows. They seemed to be staring right at the intruders.

Ian grabbed the Doctor, and began to drag him from the room. The Doctor started to protest, struggling to remain. Ian couldn't understand why – unless the Doctor didn't understand what that thing back there was. After all, the Doctor was not of the Earth. 'That's the Frankenstein monster!' Ian hissed. 'It can't be real! It's just a story, a film . . . It can't be real. *It can't be!'*

'Will you kindly stop dragging me like a sack of potatoes!' the Doctor snapped back, pulling himself free. 'If what you say is true, then there has to be some logical explanation for this.'

'And that is?'

Smoothing his collar back into place, the Doctor cleared his throat. He wanted another look at the creature, but now that he considered the matter, the thing did look rather ferocious . . . 'Well, why don't we find the ladies and see if they can shed any light on this, mmm?' In an abrupt about-face, he moved very quickly from the room. 'Come along, come along, don't dawdle!'

Ian took a last look at the creature, which was still on the table and watching him. 'I'm right behind you,' he assured the Doctor, and hastily fled the room.

The monster continued to stare at the doorway for a moment, and then it lay back down on the table. Its huge hand pulled the sheet back, until the monster was covered again. The machinery started to settle back into slumber, just like the creature. All was as it had been in the room.

Above them, from some tower in the castle, a lone bell began to peal.

In the lobby, Vicki and Barbara had finally caught their breath. As they heard the bell, they peered around the edge of the TARDIS. Thankfully, the coffin had remained shut once Barbara had dropped the lid.

'Ask not for whom the bell tolls,' she muttered softly to herself. 'I feel as though my hair has turned white.'

Vicki glanced up, and then stifled a yelp. 'It *has*!'

Alarmed, Barbara pulled a lock of hair in front of her face. It was its normal rich brown. Vicki started to giggle, and Barbara took a playful swat at her. 'One of these days . . .' she warned the teenager. 'My nerves aren't up to jokes like that.'

'I'm sorry, Barbara,' Vicki said, calming down somewhat. 'I just had to do something to break my gloomy mood.'

From behind them, a deep, resonant voice intoned: 'Good evening.'

They spun about. In the shadows, they could just make out a tall, gaunt figure and nothing more.

Essaying a tight smile, Vicki managed to answer, 'Good evening.'

'Who are you?' Barbara demanded.

In response, the figure moved forward, into the weak light. He was well over six feet tall, pale of face, but with brightly coloured lips. His eyes were intense, unblinking. A long, flowing cape, lined with red velvet, covered a dark suit and an intensely white shirt. 'My name,' he said, with a slight bow from the waist, 'is Dracula. Count Dracula.'

'You *can't* be!' Barbara exclaimed. 'Not really. Where are we, anyway?'

'Welcome to Castle Dracula,' the figure said. There was another crack of lightning and a crash of thunder, and he moved back into the shadows. After a second, Barbara followed him, only to meet smooth stone. He had vanished.

'He's . . . gone,' she whispered, feeling the stone.

'Thank goodness for that,' Vicki answered. 'He gave me the creeps.'

'There's something very wrong here,' Barbara said, trying to discover a secret panel, a hidden door – *anything* that would show her where he had gone to. He couldn't *really* have vanished . . . could he? He couldn't really be Count Dracula. There wasn't any such person! Or was there? Had the TARDIS taken them to a time when Dracula – some Dracula, at any rate – lived? She remembered that there had been

78

someone named Vlad . . . Vlad the Impaler, he'd been called. He had been a Dracula, and a real Count. Could they be in his home? 'Why did he just walk away?' she asked, as much of herself as of Vicki. 'There must be a catch here somewhere. What do you think, Vicki?'

For once, there was no sound from the youngster. Barbara glanced round, and instantly saw the reason for that.

There was no sign of Vicki anywhere in the hall.

Fighting down the panic that threatened to overwhelm her, Barbara backed away from the wall and frantically scanned the room. Vicki was nowhere to be seen. Feeling weak, Barbara collapsed into a high-backed chair near a solid-looking wall, and tried to think.

The chair spun around on a hidden hinge, as the wall section revolved. With a click, the wall had reversed itself. An identical chair now stood on the same spot as the old chair. The only difference was that this one was empty. Barbara had now vanished as well.

Ian and the Doctor came hurriedly down the stairs, glancing behind themselves as they did so. Thankfully, the creature they had seen had not followed them. Arriving in the hallway again, both men looked around. Neither Barbara nor Vicki was there.

Clicking his tongue in annoyance, the Doctor snapped, 'Now where have those young women got to?'

Ian shook his head. 'You know, there's something terribly familiar about all of this, Doctor. Yet I know I've never been here.'

'Mmm? Oh, don't be so certain of that, my boy.'

Puzzled, Ian examined the smug expression on the Doctor's face. 'Surely I'd remember a place like this if I'd seen it before.'

The Doctor waved his hand airily, dismissing the point. 'Oh, I know that *physically* you've never been here before – but *mentally* I think you've been here many times.'

'I don't understand.'

'Nor do I, fully,' the Doctor admitted. 'But it's beginning to get clearer as I think about it. You've seen old horror films, read the scary books – I saw you with that ridiculous

79

volume in the TARDIS, you know! You've had nightmares before. Monsters in haunted houses, creaking doors, thunder and lightning – and here it is, every bit of it.' He threw his arms wide to illustrate his point, almost hitting Ian with his walking stick.

Ducking, Ian tried to laugh off what the Doctor was talking about. 'Are you trying to tell me that this place exists only in my mind?'

'Oh, not just *your* mind, my boy, but in the minds of millions.' With a far-off look in his eyes, the Doctor began weaving his theory. 'Everyone who ever saw a horror film . . . All who read the works of Bram Stoker, Edgar Allan Poe, Mary Shelley . . . Everyone who tried to frighten an audience with old, dark houses, rats, bats, spiders and . . . things. All those untold horrors lurking just below the conscious mind – the fear of the unseen, the unknown, the unliving . . . It's here, all of it!'

Fighting the chain of logic that the Doctor was constructing, Ian protested: 'All of what you say may be true, but this is a *real* house.' He slapped his hand on a wall. 'It exists. It's solid.'

'Exists, yes,' the Doctor said, scornfully dismissing the facts. He tapped his temple, significantly. 'In the deepest, darkest recesses of the human mind – that's where it exists, my boy! Millions of minds, secretly believing that all of this must somehow be real. How many people, on dark nights, have heard footsteps in the blackness and imagined they were being followed by some uncanny creature? How many people have walked into haunted houses, defying the spirits – and all the time secretly afraid that they would confront the unknown and unknowable? The immense power of their fears, their beliefs, their nightmares – that has made this place a reality! A house of horrors, yanked from the deepest recesses of the human mind!'

'You mean . . .' Ian struggled to follow the Doctor's poetic soaring, 'you mean that we've strayed into some strange nether world – neither real nor unreal – an illusion, a *belief* so powerful that it actually exists?'

'Precisely,' the Doctor beamed, patting Ian's hand

condescendingly. 'When you think about it, it's all so logical. What do they train your minds on in those vaunted English schools of yours?'

Ignoring the insult, Ian smiled. 'Then we're safe, Doctor.'

'Safe? Haven't you heard a word I've been saying? How can we be safe here in a dimension of nightmares?'

'Don't you see?' Ian asked, eagerly. 'If this is a realm made from the frightened dreams of *men*, then the Daleks can't land here, can they?'

The Doctor was astonished, and then pleased. 'You know, I do believe you're right, my boy. Perhaps they do teach something worth while at Coal Hill School after all! The Daleks could never land here. Never!' Gripping his lapels, he preened himself happily, certain of his chain of logic.

Unfortunately for the Doctor and his companions, reality was not quite as accommodating as the Doctor's beliefs indicated. In the next room, with its soft whine, the Dalek time machine materialized.

9

Fallen Spirits

The Patrol Leader turned with satisfaction from the screens inside the time machine. 'The scanners indicate that the enemy time machine is still here. We have caught them.'

'Which planet are we on?' The Second-in-command asked.

'Earth. They have changed their geographical and temporal location by only a few units.'

'They cannot elude us this time.'

'No.' The Leader moved away from the controls. 'Disembark the search force.'

The Daleks began to glide out of their time machine, ready to seek out their foes. Following the instructions of the Leader, they dispersed to look through the dark corridors and rooms. Unlike their four targets, the Daleks had no innate fear of either the shadows or the unknown. If something existed, it could be destroyed; if it did not exist, then it was of no importance. They also had, naturally, no knowledge of the creatures of human myths and imagination.

Exploring upstairs, one of the Daleks came upon the laboratory. Scanning the area showed one humanoid figure, stretched out on a table. Moving forward to investigate, the Dalek passed between the large tubes.

Instantly, the rings of light began to float upwards, inside the vacuum tubes. The Dalek spun about, seeking for whoever had triggered the machinery. There was still no one in sight but the unmoving figure on the table. Switching to infra-red, the Dalek saw that a low-level photoelectric eye had been set up between the tubes. Passing through the beam had set the machinery into motion.

The light-tubes had built up to their peak again, and the twin globes moved over the sheeted figure. A blast of electricity sizzled through the air, and then the being on the table began to stir. The Dalek had no interest in the appearance of the creature – all humanoids looked equally ugly to it – but it was displaying some form of intelligence, even though it was not registering as a living being.

'Halt!' the Dalek grated. 'You will answer my questions!'

Ignoring the order, the Frankenstein monster pushed back the sheet, and sat up, swinging its legs to the floor. Evidently, the creature would not obey. The Dalek opened fire at it. In the stream of radiation, the monster seemed totally untouched. Then it simply lay down again and covered itself.

The Dalek was worried over the immunity this being showed to the lethal radiation fire. No living creature was supposed to be able to withstand a sustained burst as this creature had. Before the Dalek could reach the logical conclusion, a bell began to peal hollowly from some floor above. The Dalek whirled about, and set off to investigate.

Blissfully unaware of how wrong his conclusions were, the Doctor was once again feeling confident. As usual, this made him smug and garrulous. Ian had difficulty in getting him to listen, but then reminded him that Barbara and Vicki were still missing.

'Where can they have gone to?' he asked. 'We would have seen them if they had gone upstairs. And they certainly didn't want to get too far away from the TARDIS.'

'Listen!' the Doctor interrupted him, holding up a hand. 'There's somebody coming, Chesterton.' He gestured towards the door leading from the room to the rest of the castle. 'Behind there.'

Before they could move, something hit the door hard. The solid oak cracked, split and showered all over the floor. The bulk of it simply collapsed forwards. In the door frame stood a Dalek, scanning the room. As it saw Ian and the Doctor, its gun came into firing position.

'Get under cover!' Ian yelled, propelling the Doctor

towards the stairs. Both of them ducked behind the stonework as the Dalek fired. It had had no time to reset its weapon from the broad-spectrum energy blast used on the door to the killing radiation beam. Curtains over one of the windows burst into flames from the force of the blast, casting an eerie red glow over the room.

The Doctor tapped Ian on the arm and pointed. The TARDIS door was facing away from the shattered door. 'We have to get back to the TARDIS,' he hissed. 'It will protect us while we enter.'

Ian nodded, and peered round the edge of the stairs. The Dalek was trying to move the door out of its way on the floor so that it could enter the room after them. While it was so occupied, Ian led the Doctor in a sprint for the TARDIS. The Dalek reacted, but by the time it could fire again, they were safely under the cover of the TARDIS, which absorbed the blast without any apparent ill effects. The Doctor fished hastily in his pocket for the key.

'So there you are!'

Ian and the Doctor spun around, to see a wall panel opening beside the TARDIS. Barbara and Vicki, both covered in dust and cobwebs, emerged, brushing at their hair and clothing.

'Where have you been?' the Doctor snapped, testily.

Vicki grinned. 'We stumbled into these really weird tunnels, hidden in this place and—'

'Tell us later,' Ian broke in, pushing the Doctor back to the TARDIS door. 'The Daleks are here, and we've got to move fast!'

Vicki glanced around in horror, then screamed: 'Look out!'

The Dalek that had been examining the laboratory had now reached the top of the stairs. From there, it had a perfectly clear field of fire at the TARDIS doors. At the same moment, the Dalek in the doorway finally pushed its way into the room, moving grimly towards the TARDIS.

The second Dalek was the closer of the two. The one upstairs waited. Vicki dived for cover, just as the Doctor finally succeeded in fumbling the TARDIS doors open. The second Dalek triggered another of the photoelectric beams, and a panel behind it in the wall opened. Fearing an ambush, the Dalek spun about.

A shadowy figure moved forward. 'Good evening,' it said, in hollow tones.

While the Dalek was distracted, Ian pushed at the Doctor and Barbara. 'Inside!' he snapped. 'It's our only chance!'

The Doctor peered around for Vicki. She was nowhere in sight. Believing that she had already entered, the Doctor followed the other two in and slammed the doors.

As Dracula moved forwards to greet the Dalek, he was met by a burst of fire. The blast had no effect at all. 'My name is Dracula. Count Dracula.' He bowed slightly from the waist. 'Welcome to Castle Dracula.'

'Stay back! Stay back!' the Dalek grated, firing again. It was in a state of near-panic, as its lethal radiation blasts seemed to be having absolutely no effect on the humanoid. The Dalek at the top of the stairs joined in the firing. Alerted by the noise, more Daleks came into the room.

Such was the state of the battle with Dracula that none of them saw when the TARDIS dematerialized. The only eyes that watched belonged to Vicki, crouching behind the stairs. In sheer disbelief and horror, she realized that her friends must have believed she was already safely inside. Instead, she was stuck here, in this terrible house, with monsters and Daleks.

The one thing that she dared not do was to panic. There had to be some way to rejoin the Doctor. There had to be! Fighting down the urge simply to scream and run, she forced herself to consider her options. with the TARDIS gone, there was only one way out of this horrible place – but it was a case of out of the frying pan and into the fire . . . Screwing up all of her courage, she began moving towards the doorway.

Intent on Dracula, the Daleks didn't see her move. Instead, several more of them began firing at this creature that refused to die. Finally, something happened, though not what the Daleks had wanted. The figure seemed to stiffen, then moved jerkily forwards. 'I am . . . I am . . .' it slurred. Both hands came up, as it walked towards the closest Dalek, ignoring the firing. 'Dracula!' it finished. His hands collided blindly with the Dalek, then began tearing at it.

'Help me!' the Dalek screamed, attempting unsuccessfully to retreat. 'Help me!' Dracula tore off its eyestick, then began to rip at the casing itself. In a shower of sparks, the Dalek exploded, its power systems disrupted. The blast knocked Dracula back, shredding his clothing and burning at his chest.

Instead of flesh and blood, this exposed gears and wiring. 'I am . . . I am . . .' Dracula continued, moving randomly around, as though looking for another victim. The Daleks backed away.

The lone Dalek at the head of the stairs did not see the creature lumbering through the shadows behind it until too late. The Frankenstein monster had emerged from the laboratory, moving with unsteady steps. Finally, it groaned, and crashed into the back of the Dalek, propelling the Dalek straight down the steps. As it fell, the Dalek tumbled, spun and finally crashed into the floor. Badly damaged, it then exploded.

The monster did not stop, but continued down the steps. It was unsteady, but somehow managed to traverse them without toppling over. It then advanced on the Daleks from one side, as the damaged Dracula moved forward on the other.

'Retreat! Retreat!' the Dalek Leader called. 'The enemy is resistant to our fire.' The rest of the squad needed no further encouragement to evacuate the room. Two Daleks were finished and still burning, sending up a cloud of smoke. From this cloud, Dracula and the Frankenstein monster continued their slow, unsteady advance.

The Daleks returned to their time machine, and sealed the doors. The Leader examined the screens, and grated, 'The enemy time machine has departed. Prepare to follow!'

'I obey!' The other Daleks moved to their positions, and began to power up the time computers. Again, the Doctor had escaped them – but they were now much closer. The next time, they would succeed in exterminating him!

Leaning against the TARDIS doors, Ian mopped his brow

with the back of his sleeve. 'Phew!' he exclaimed, loudly. 'This game of hide and seek through time is getting a little wearing.'

The Doctor glanced up from the controls, as he ensured that the TARDIS was correctly in flight. 'Well, at least it has given us the unique experience of seeing the meeting of colossi – Frankenstein's monster versus the Daleks!' He chuckled at the thought.

Barbara, standing beside the Doctor, looked puzzled. 'Frankenstein?' she echoed, 'But he's just a fictional character.'

Moving across to join them, Ian smiled. 'I know he's *supposed* to be fictional, Barbara, but the Doctor has a theory to explain what we saw.'

'A theory?' the Doctor sounded insulted. 'Well, call it what you like, but I personally am convinced that the castle we were in exists in neither time nor space. Somehow, for some reason, we were lodged for a brief period of time in a place that exists only in the human mind. The realm of the imagination!'

Barbara suddenly realized what the Doctor meant. 'That place was just the . . . the solidified dreams and nightmares of human beings?'

'Exactly.' The Doctor looked insufferably pleased with himself.

'Well, I for one don't believe a word of it,' Ian announced. 'If that were the case, how could the Daleks have landed there? *They* can't invade human thoughts.'

The Doctor sniffed, loudly. 'I refuse to argue with a closed mind, Chesterton.' He turned his back on Ian and bent over the controls again.

'Have it your own way,' Ian laughed. 'But I'm certain there has to be another, *logical* explanation.'

(Ian was quite correct; had the travellers gone out through the main doors of the castle, they would have seen that there was neither thunder nor lightning outside. A bright, April day led the crowds through Battersea Funfair. Standing by the castle was a sign: 'The House of Frankenstein: Admission – ' The price was obliterated by a second sign reading: 'Closed for repairs'.)

Refusing to contribute to what might turn into another of those ongoing arguments between the Doctor and Ian, Barbara looked around. 'Have you seen Vicki?' she asked.

Ian was moving towards the door that led to the rest of the TARDIS. 'Mmm? Oh, I expect she's in her room, changing.' He sniffed at his sweater. 'Come to think of it, that's not a bad idea. Running through haunted houses does work up a sweat.'

'I'll go and make sure she's all right, Barbara said, and left. Ian was about to follow when a thought struck him. he turned back to the Doctor.

'Any sign yet of the Dalek ship?'

The Doctor glanced up, uneasily. 'Yes, it's just begun to register now. I'm afraid they're on our trail again.'

'We can't go on running like this!' Ian exclaimed, slamming his fist into the door frame. 'We might give them the slip once or twice more, but sooner or later we have to face them.'

Straightening up, the Doctor nodded glumly. 'Yes, I'm afraid that running away will solve nothing. Each time we've landed I've hoped for conditions that would allow us to take a stand and fight the Daleks. When we do face them finally, Chesterton, it'll be with no turning back. There'll be no quarter given – it'll be us or them.

Before Ian could respond, Barbara came running back into the room, on the verge of panic. 'She's not here! I've looked everywhere – Vicki's not here!'

Three pairs of eyes turned to the time rotor as it rose and fell. They all knew that leaving Vicki behind in the haunted house might well have signed her death warrant . . .

The Dalek Leader turned to its assistant. The second Dalek looked round from the panel it was checking in the control room. 'We are locked on to pursuit course,' it reported.

'Calculate destination of the enemy time machine,' the Leader ordered.

Turning back to the panel, the technician Dalek began to compute the course that they were locked into. The fluxes of the Vortex made such tracking difficult, but not impossible. With typical Dalek determination, their computers had been constructed to perform the complex calculations. Finally, the technician's eyestick focused on the Patrol Leader. 'It will land next on the planet Mechanus.'

'Understood. Contact Skaro Control and report our destination to the Dalek Supreme.'

'I obey.' The technician moved into an alcove at the rear of the control room. In it was a very powerful sub-space tachyon transmitter. Normal forms of communication were impossible while in transit through the Space/Time Vortex. The tachyon beamer could break through the fields of static and generally reach its target with a tight transmission. The technician began to adjust the controls to send the message.

The Leader glided to a small room at the back of the control room. It was one of the two laboratories that the time ship was fitted with. One of the Dalek scientists had remained here throughout the flight, preparing the unit in the room. It was a transparent box on a raised dais. This was linked to a large bank of controls that the scientist was carefully adjusting. It was checking the settings against a read-out on one of the ship's computers. As the Leader arrived, the scientist spun its head about, continuing its manipulations as it spoke.

'Which of the four enemy is to be reproduced?'

'Their leader,' the Patrol Leader answered. 'The one they call *Doctor*. Is the replicator programmed?'

The scientist moved towards the transparent box, which was just over six feet long. Using its sucker-stick, the scientist manipulated another control. The glass coloration darkened, then solidified. Within the box was a vaguely humanoid form, though without features or definition. 'All is ready,' the Dalek reported. 'Our data files have been analysed and the computers are prepared to begin. By the time that we reach our destination, the machine will have taken all of the data and built a perfect duplicate of the one called *Doctor*.'

'Good.' The Leader spun about to leave, then swivelled its head about. 'Commence operations, and then join me in the command post.'

'I obey.' As the Leader left, the scientist finished its operations with the machinery. The translucent box began to pulsate with colours. Satisfied, the scientist also left the room. The planned reproduction was under way.

After a moment, Vicki peered warily out from behind a panel of instruments. With the Daleks distracted fighting the monsters in the haunted house, she had seized her chance to slip into their ship. Sooner or later, she was bound to meet with the Doctor and the others again – if the Daleks didn't discover her first. Biting back that thought, she glanced about the room she was in. She had no option but to hope that everything would turn out all right.

She crossed to the replicator, and looked at it in puzzlement. She had heard what the Daleks had talked about, but found it hard to believe that this machine could create a duplicate of anyone. The screens at the base showed images of the Doctor from various angles, animated by the computers. Vicki knew that the Doctor had met and defeated the Daleks twice before. Obviously, then, the Daleks had made visual records of him at those times. No, more than records – they must have *studied* him in detail if they were hoping to create a copy. Vicki wished she knew how to stop the machine before it could finish its task – and then realized that if she were to sabotage it somehow, this would reveal to the Daleks that there was a stowaway on board. If they suspected this for an instant, then she would be found and killed.

Returning to the panel she had hidden behind, she discovered that it was a sub-space transmitter, similar to the one in the control room. Obviously, it was for use when the scientist Dalek needed to access files back on Skaro. Vicki had been trained during her enforced stay on the planet Dido in the use and theory of transmitters not too different to this. Though the Doctor had rescued her, the memory of her weeks and months listening for a rescue ship at the radio equipment was still fresh in her mind. She checked the board, one eye carefully watching for the return of any Daleks. Signal amplifier, tuner, power boost, microphone . . . She traced each with her hand, making sure she could operate the machine – and then return it to its present settings afterwards. Finally, her hands flew over the controls, as she fine-tuned it to one setting. Then she paused, as a sudden thought struck her: did the TARDIS have a radio receiver?

She had never *seen* one, but then again, there was a great deal of the TARDIS she simply had not had a chance to explore. In fact, even in the control room, many of the instruments that she had seen puzzled her. One of them *had* to be a radio, surely? Who would build a ship that didn't have one? She tried to fight down a voice that told her the Doctor would be quite likely to do such a foolish thing.

There was only one possible wavelength that she could think of to transmit on – 21 centimetres. The chances that the Doctor would have a radio on and listening for a message would be slim – but *all* ships that Vicki knew of had automatic scanners that monitored this frequency – the frequency of the hydrogen atoms in free space, the commonest element of all in the Universe. A modulated signal at that precise wavelength was standard for all distress calls. Praying that the TARDIS at least had such instruments, Vicki started the radio transmitting, and whispered into the microphone: 'Hello TARDIS! Hello TARDIS. Can you hear me? Over.' She switched to receiving. Nothing but static. She tried again. Once more, no reply.

The sound of the replicator suddenly cut out, leaving only the background electronic heartbeat of the Dalek ship. Curious, she moved over to take another wary look. The box was again fully transparent, and within it lay a very familiar figure – the Doctor! His eyes were closed, as though sleeping, his hands clenched over the silver head of his cane. His clothing, the ring on his finger – even the lines in his face and the thin, long white hair – they were all exactly as they were in the real Doctor!

The Doctor himself was far from sleeping peacefully. He was striding back and forth in the TARDIS control room, muttering loudly to himself. 'It's my fault! My stupid, stupid fault! I should never have moved the TARDIS without being absolutely certain that we were all aboard. I shall never forgive myself! Never!'

Ian interrupted the Doctor's pacing. 'No, Doctor, we're all equally to blame. I assumed that Vicki was in the ship too.'

'Isn't there anything we can do?' Barbara asked. The strain was showing on them all. Barbara was drained, pale and exhausted. The others were no better. 'Is there no way of going back for her?'

'Do you think I'd just be standing here doing nothing if there were?' the Doctor yelled. 'We're completely helpless. You – you, of all people, should know how impossible it is to pilot the TARDIS back to one space and time!' He didn't add that he had been trying to get the two teachers home now for several years' subjective time. Each attempt had failed.

'Yes, but that's because we've never stayed in one spot long enough to repair all of the TARDIS's systems,' Ian exclaimed. 'Even when we first met you, back in Totter's Lane, the TARDIS was in need of repairs. Since then . . . well, you have let the repairs slip a bit. If we had the time and the facilities, do you think we could find our way back again?'

The Doctor considered this for a moment, then shook his head. 'Possibly, possibly,' he sighed. He gestured to the computers behind the glass wall. 'All of our flight information is recorded in those. Theoretically, if all of the TARDIS's systems were functioning as they should, it would be child's play to retrace our steps. But that could take months . . . years . . . *If* we could find the right tools to repair the ship. And *if* my memory of the correct settings and everything is a hundred per cent reliable.'

Barbara moved forwards, an anxious expression on her face. If the Doctor gave up, then there was no hope at all for Vicki. 'But if all of us worked on it and helped – wouldn't it be worth a try?'

'Of course it would, yes.' The Doctor glared at her. 'But do you think that the Daleks are just going to sit back and give us the time to tinker with the TARDIS? They're after us to *kill* us, not to play a game of cricket, you know!'

'The Daleks!' Ian's face lit up, and he slapped his fist into the palm of his other hand. 'That's it! Doctor, don't you see? They're our answer.' Both of his friends had blank expressions. 'We can get back to Vicki! Not in the TARDIS – *but in the Daleks' time machine!*'

Finally getting the idea, the Doctor's frown vanished as a smile washed over his face. 'Capture their machine?' he asked, in dawning comprehension.

'Yes, why not?'

'It'll take some doing,' Barbara snorted.

'But it's the only chance we've got of getting back to Vicki. We know that the Daleks' ship is fully controllable.'

'If we can only pull it off,' the Doctor mused, seeking inspiration.

Barbara looked from one to the other. 'Well, it seems to me that we have nothing to lose,' she said, firmly. 'As Ian keeps reminding us, we can't run forever. Now we have even more reason to stop and fight.'

Ian turned to the Doctor. 'Well, what do you say?'

'I say – yes!' Resolved, the Doctor scuttled back to the control console. 'Yes, yes, yes! The Daleks have hounded us for quite long enough. Wherever we land next will be our battleground. Either we shall win, or they shall – but it will be finally decided!'

Vicki backed away from the replication machine, unable to tear her eyes away from the figure that looked so much like the Doctor. She bumped into the radio panel, but before she could begin to send her signal again, she heard an approaching Dalek. Quickly, she reset the controls, then ducked back behind the panel.

The Dalek Leader and the scientist returned to the room. Behind them came a third Dalek, which moved to the radio panel Vicki had just vacated.

'Report the position of the enemy time machine,' the Leader ordered.

The Dalek at the panel checked the controls. 'Its movement through time is ending. It is now approaching the planet Mechanus.'

'How long before we arrive?'

'Four units.'

The Leader turned to the scientist. 'Is the robot completed?'

The scientist had been examining the replicator's controls. 'Affirmative. The computers are now feeding data to its memory cells. Physical duplication is completed. Energy cells are fully charged. The brain unit is almost complete with characteristics and personality traits.'

The Leader grated: 'Prepare to activate.'

Closing a switch, the scientist began the process. The coffin-like structure housing the duplicate Doctor started to rise to the vertical. As it did so, the instrumentation scanned the apparently sleeping form for any flaws or malfunctions. Nothing showed adversely on the screens. The front panel then slid soundlessly downwards, exposing the robot.

'Activate!' the Leader ordered.

The scientist moved the final controls. The three Dalek eyes and Vicki's two human ones stared at the robot, waiting.

Its eyes abruptly opened, and it looked back at them.

The time rotor stopped its rise and fall, as with its usual wheezing and complaining the TARDIS finished its journey. The Doctor activated the scanner, and they looked out at the battlefield that fate had selected for them. Here they would face the Daleks.

After a moment, Ian observed: 'It looks a bit swampy.'

It did indeed. Mists wreathed the ground and, in the dim half-light of evening, this limited visibility considerably. Tall growths were covered in what appeared to be vines. Pools of water were visible, indicating the nature of the area. There was no sign of animal life.

'All to the good,' the Doctor answered. 'This sort of terrain should make it difficult for the Daleks, mm?'

'Well, we don't have much time,' Ian said, practically. 'We'd better start exploring before the Daleks do arrive.'

'One moment!' the Doctor cautioned, as he completed his environmental checks. 'Mmm . . . Well, however it may

look, it seems to be perfectly safe for us to venture outside.'
He activated the door switch, and the double doors hummed
open. As they did, a rancid smell filled the room.

'Phew!' Ian exclaimed. 'Well, it smells like a swamp, too.'
They ventured out of the TARDIS and looked around as the
Doctor carefully closed and locked the doors.

As they watched, they could see that some of the overhanging
tendrils were twitching, and then these began moving slowly
towards the three new arrivals.

'Look at that!' Barbara exclaimed, pointing. One frond was
creeping quite visibly down the bole of some huge, multi-rooted
tree.

'You realize what that must mean, don't you?' the Doctor
asked coldly. 'No plants have to move that fast if they feed
by photosynthesis. They have to be carnivores – and I suspect
that it's our flesh they want to sample!'

The Dalek Leader moved forward to examine the robot,
comparing it to the read-out panel of the computer. As it did
so, all of its movements were followed by the piercing eyes of
the duplicate Doctor. Finally, the Leader swivelled back to the
scientist. 'It is impossible to distinguish from the original.'

At the panel, the third Dalek lifted its eyestick. 'We have
landed on the planet Mechanus,' it reported.

Spinning its head around, the Leader ordered: 'Assassination
squad to prepare to disembark.' Refocusing on the scientist,
it added: 'Activate the mobility unit for the robot.'

The scientist did so, and moved away from the robot. The
replicated Doctor then came smoothly from the glass case, and
stood, looking over its creators.

The Leader faced it. 'Your orders are understood? You will
infiltrate and kill . . . Infiltrate and kill.'

'Understand?' The voice was perfectly like that of the Doctor.
'My dear fellow, of course I understand. Don't *fuss* so!' It waved
its hand in a gesture only too familiar to the hidden observer.
'I shall infiltrate and kill. Quite so, quite so.'

Vicki was horrified. The robot was all too perfect . . . It was
behaving exactly as the real Doctor would . . .

10

Who's Who?

As they looked about the jungle they had landed in, Ian, Barbara and the Doctor all felt extremely uneasy. Whenever they stood still for a moment to catch their breath, the vines would begin moving towards them, their tips quivering as if they could scent their prey. When the travellers moved on, there were all kinds of shuffling noises paralleling their path – noises that ceased when they did, and resumed when they started out again.

One particularly nauseating plant looked like an eight-foot tall mushroom with creepers stuck to the edges of its cap. It appeared to be firmly rooted in place, but the creepers were in constant motion. One of them had caught what looked like a tiny rat with six legs. The squealing creature was borne aloft, struggling, to vanish within the large cap. Then the creeper reappeared, empty.

'What is it, Doctor?' Barbara asked, shuddering.

'I don't know,' he answered. 'Some sort of fungoid growth, I expect. On Earth, many fungi feed on decaying remains, you know.'

'Yes,' Ian observed grimly. 'And on this world, these fungoids seem to have taken that a step further – they feed on the remains while they're still alive. I expect if we got too close to one of those things, it'd be having us for supper.'

'I don't like to ask,' Barbara said, nervously backing into Ian, 'but isn't the jungle closer to us now than when we first landed?'

Ian had no chance to reply. The darkness was getting deeper, but suddenly twin rows of lights sprang to glaring brilliance. The travellers blinked, shielding their eyes from the sudden intensity. The two rows were straight and parallel, set about six feet apart. They were standing in the middle of the twin lines, which led in one direction back towards the TARDIS. In the other . . . ?

As the lights flashed on, there was a squeaking sound from the plants. The incoming wall of vegetation stopped, and then began a slow, reluctant retreat.

'Our friends don't like the light, obviously,' the Doctor chuckled.

'Yes.' Ian tried to follow the dazzling pathway, but could see little for the glare from the path and the impenetrable blackness of the jungle. 'What I want to know is who switched them on – and why they were placed here.'

'Does it matter?' Barbara asked, anxiously. 'Just so long as they stay on. We can get back to the TARDIS now.'

'No, no, no,' the Doctor interrupted. 'It *is* important. It suggests that there is intelligence of some kind on this planet.'

'There's a definite pathway through the swamp,' Ian pointed out. 'A corridor of light.'

'Yes, quite – a definite pattern. As you say, Chesterton, a corridor.' The Doctor looked at them both, and the gleam in his eye wasn't purely from the lights; the Doctor loved nothing as much as a mystery to be solved. 'I suggest that we follow it.'

'*Follow it?*' Barbara echoed, incredulously.

'Yes, of course.' Seeing that Barbara was less than enthusiastic, the Doctor donned a conciliatory air. 'Our plan was to capture the Dalek time machine and then return for Vicki, remember? Nothing's changed – and it may be that at the end of this . . . this handiwork of civilization, we may find friends or allies to help us to defeat the Daleks. After all, they have already stopped us from becoming the first course for a mushroom! Now come along – and remember, it's highly probable that the Daleks have already landed here . . .'

Without looking back, he set off down the path. Barbara glanced helplessly at Ian, shrugged, and followed after. Ian, looking over his shoulder from time to time, brought up the rear. Despite the Doctor's optimism, he couldn't help but wonder if the lights were switched on to save them – or simply because it was night-time. Perhaps the native intelligences of this world would not be as benevolent as the Doctor seemed to think.

The Daleks had indeed landed, not too far from the TARDIS. In their metal shells, they were not as tempting titbits for the local flora as the humans had been. As a result, the jungle was less thick about the Dalek time machine. From the entrance to the machine, the Dalek Leader surveyed the area. Its infra-red vision helped it to see perfectly in the night. All looked relatively peaceful. The Leader turned to the scientist.

'Is the replica Doctor ready?'

'Yes. It awaits your commands.'

On cue, the robot Doctor came from within the craft, and looked about. It sniffed, obviously finding the surroundings unappealing.

'Our enemies are moving through the jungle,' the Leader reported. With its infra-red vision, it would be able to see their prints clearly on the muddy jungle floor, once their time machine was discovered. 'You are to join them.'

'Yes, yes, yes,' the robot said, impatiently. 'Infiltrate and kill, infiltrate and kill. I understand perfectly. Well, the sooner I get started, the sooner I shall accomplish my mission, mmm?' Waving his cane cheerily, it set off down the pathway after the three travellers.

Turning to two other Daleks, the Leader ordered: 'Follow it as escorts, but remain out of sight until it has made contact. The rest of the patrol will seek out the enemy time machine in case the humans elude the robot.'

Under the Leader's instructions, the Daleks began to deploy throughout the jungle. For a moment, the space about the Dalek ship was still. Then Vicki peered cautiously around the doorway of the time machine. Seeing that the path was clear, she set off after the robot Doctor. She had to find and warn her friends!

*

The Doctor, Ian and Barbara were progressing down the light pathway. Fired on by his enthusiasm, the Doctor was making good time. Barbara was doing less well, and she stumbled again over something in her way. Before she could fall, Ian grabbed and held her firmly. Aware that he was ahead, the Doctor turned impatiently.

'Come along, come along!' he snapped. 'Don't dawdle.'

Laughing, Ian gestured for him to start on again. He and Barbara then followed.

A moment later, the robot Doctor stepped out of the jungle. It had been untouched by the predatory vegetation, and had made good time. Watching carefully, it then set off along the pathway after its prey. It was intent on the chase, and unaware that it was being followed in its turn. Vicki was moving cautiously after it, unaware of the lethal nature of the plant life. As she saw one of the Dalek patrol, she backed into hiding. Unfortunately, she had chosen badly.

The fungoid was waiting, almost eagerly, as a large piece of food moved into its fringes. It was perhaps a trifle too eager. As Vicki moved backwards, its tentacles lashed out. Two caught the young girl. With a squeal, Vicki tore free, stumbling to her knees. If a fungoid could be said to have emotions, this one showed every sign of frustration. Like snakes, its tentacles whipped back and forth. On her hands and knees, Vicki scrambled back on to the path before straightening and then continuing after the robot, shaking with fear.

The lights led into a cave, and then stopped. The final few lights were set into the cave walls. The opening was large, and the cave was about twenty feet deep, and ten tall. There were rocks scattered about, and a raised section to one side, roughly three feet above the general floor. As Ian and Barbara arrived, the Doctor was already poking about. He looked up at them.

'Our corridor of lights has ended,' he announced dramatically, as if he were responsible for this miracle.

Ian picked up a small rock and started to tap the walls.

They all sounded alike. 'Seems solid enough,' he commented. 'But why would anyone arrange such an elaborate system of lighting, just to lead into a cave?

Barbara was looking about behind the rocks, and straightened with a cry of triumph. 'Over here!' As the Doctor and Ian came across to join her, she showed them what she had discovered. It was a rod about three feet in length. The end she was holding was thicker, obviously a handle. On it was a small box and a button. She pressed this, and a bright light shone from the end of the rod. Grinning, she showed it to her friends. 'There's more back there,' she informed them. She handed hers to the Doctor and took up another for herself, passing a third to Ian.

He examined it for a moment, puzzled. 'What do you make of it, Doctor?'

'A weapon, Chesterton, a weapon!' Chuckling, the Doctor triggered his rod, and the brilliant light issued from its end. 'Don't you see what its purpose is?'

'To be honest, no.'

The Doctor shook his head, sadly. 'My dear boy, your lack of perception distresses me greatly on occasions. Never mind, never mind.'

Barbara's face lit up. 'They're designed to scare off those fungoid things we saw in the swamp!'

Patting her arm condescendingly, the Doctor smiled. 'Very good, my dear – excellent! Of course that's what they are. Really, Chesterton, you should have guessed. High-intensity light, to scare off those plant creatures.'

Ian looked up at the roof, with a feigned expression of long-suffering. 'When you've both finished revelling in my ignorance, perhaps you can tell me what we're to do next?'

Airily, the Doctor dismissed the problem. 'Well, if we're to capture the Dalek time machine, our first task is obviously to locate it.'

Shuddering, Barbara added, 'And that means going back into the swamp again.'

'Yes.' The Doctor held up his rod. 'But now we've got some sort of defence.' He started to wave the stick like a sword.

'They might keep the fungoids at bay,' Ian commented, 'but they do have a disadvantage.'

Pausing, the Doctor asked: 'And what might that be?'

Seizing his chance, Ian grinned. 'Really, Doctor, on occasions your lack of perception distresses me greatly.'

For all his faults, the Doctor could accept being the brunt of a joke. 'Mmm—I do believe that the word is *touché.*'

Barbara wasn't as patient. 'When you've quite finished acting like a pair of politicians at the polls, will you tell me what the problem is?'

'If we flash these things about to scare off the fungoids,' Ian observed, 'then we'll give our position away to the Daleks.'

'A good point,' the Doctor conceded.

'But what about the light path?' Barbara said. She gestured to the mouth of the cave. 'It's a dead giveaway, leading right to this cave as it does.'

'Quite right, quite right.' The Doctor put down his rod. 'We dare not advertise our position. I think the best thing we can do is to wait here till the morning.'

'And the outside lights?' Ian asked.

'We had best look around and see if we can find the cable that supplies their power. If we can break it, we should be fairly safe.' He started to search, and Ian and Barbara joined him in his exploration. After a few minutes, Barbara called them over. She had found the wiring, buried under the thin layer of sand in the cave.

Ian gripped the wire, and tested it. 'It's tough . . .' Reaching into his pocket, he pulled out a pocket knife. Using this, he sawed through the strand.

Outside, the lights died abruptly, and the whole area went black.

Vicki stood still, as the darkness closed in about her. While the lights had been on, she had felt fairly confident. Now, in the darkness, she froze in fear. She could see nothing, but she could hear too much . . . Rustlings, creakings, rattling sounds . . . All about, it seemed that the jungle was on the move again.

101

She was perhaps braver than most people would be, but this was simply too much for her. The scream began deep within her, breaking out loudly. She lost her nerve completely, and fell to the jungle floor, covering her head and wishing against all hope that everything would just go away and leave her in peace.

The vegetation started to creep towards her . . .

In the cave, the three travellers stiffened. They had heard the scream perfectly.

'There's someone out there!' Ian exclaimed. Grabbing two of the light sticks, he thrust one at the Doctor. 'Come on – quickly!'

'Yes, yes, of course,' the Doctor agreed, looking none too happy at the thought of venturing into the jungle, even with his light weapon.

'Barbara,' Ian called over his shoulder. 'Stay here!' He and the Doctor vanished into the blackness, their sticks' tips glowing for a moment before they were swallowed into the dark. Barbara took up her stick again, and lit it. It seemed a very feeble defence against the horrors without the cave.

The Daleks had been thrown into some confusion as the lights died. Then they switched back to infra-red. The jungle was perfectly clear to them again.

'Patrols will continue to advance,' the Leader ordered. 'Perceptors show movement in the area ahead.'

A second Dalek moved past to follow the path. As it did so, it ventured too close to a fungoid. The vegetable brain the thing possessed was too feeble to realize that the animal life it sensed was housed within metal. Its fronds slapped down, gripping the Dalek and dragging it backwards. It could not lift the creature – it was too heavy – so it simply lowered its cap.

The Dalek was not immediately concerned until the first of the digestive juices secreted by the fungoid spattered on to its casing. They were of concentrated acid, and with hissing sounds began to eat through the metal.

'Assist! Assist!' the Dalek called, in near panic. It was being held too firmly in the tentacles to bring its gun to bear.

The Patrol Leader spun and fired. The fungoid caught fire, and instantly released its prey. It withered, collapsed and died.

'Continue the patrol,' the Leader ordered. The Dalek, its casing scarred with the acid burns, moved off.

Ian broke through the already overgrown pathway, seeing a figure stretched unconscious in the darkness. He waved his stick at the vegetation closing in. Reluctantly, the fronds and tentacles backed off, and Ian could see who it was he had saved.

'Vicki!' he cried. 'Vicki!'

The Doctor had caught up with him. 'She must have stowed away aboard the Dalek time machine, Chesterton!' he exclaimed. 'Which means that they can't be far away!'

Barbara had tired of waiting, and set to work being useful. Picking up the end of the wire that Ian had cut through, she followed it back, hoping to discover another way from the cave. Instead, the wiring vanished into a small hole in the roof. Using the stick, she could just reach the rock there, and started to tap at it. Was there a hollow section?

Suddenly, she was aware that there was someone else present. Looking around, she saw with relief that it was the Doctor. 'That was quick,' she commented.

'Mmm?' He looked at her with unusual concentration. 'Yes, yes, I was.'

'Who was it?' When the Doctor looked blank, she added: 'The scream?'

'Oh, that. Oh, um, nothing, no one.'

Puzzled at this odd series of responses, Barbara walked over to the entrance. 'Well, where's Ian, then?' The Doctor did not reply, and Barbara was worried. 'What's wrong? Where's Ian?'

The Doctor looked up, and said softly, 'Barbara, my dear . . . I . . .' He spread his hands. 'Chesterton is dead.'

103

'*Dead*?' Barbara whispered, not believing it. 'Dead?' She felt giddy and sick, and reeled back against the cave wall to support herself. Then she buried her face in her hands and began to cry. She couldn't even imagine not seeing Ian's cheerful face again, or not knowing that he was close when danger threatened. On Aridius, she had thought that she had felt as terrible as she ever would; this time it was even worse. She had allowed herself some secret reserve of hope before, but now the Doctor himself was claiming that Ian had perished. If Ian had died, how could she go on?

The Doctor put an arm about her, patting her comfortingly. His face, which she could not see, showed no such emotion: it held only triumph and a superior sneer. 'We are no longer safe here,' he said, gently. 'We must get away.'

Faced with the prospect of doing something, however pointless, Barbara began to drag her tattered spirit back together. 'But . . . Ian . . . are you *sure*? Maybe he's just hurt, and lying out there needing help . . .'

'He was dead, Barbara. The plants got him. There was nothing that I could do, but it was over quickly. Now, come along. We must hurry.' The Doctor steered her towards the entrance. Uncaring, Barbara stumbled along, and went with the Doctor into the darkness.

After a few more minutes, light was evident along the pathway. Up a gentle incline to the cave came Ian, carrying the unconscious Vicki in his arms. Behind him, waving the two light sticks at anything that moved, the Doctor followed, puffing and panting.

'Nearly there, Doctor,' Ian called over his shoulder. 'Another twenty yards.'

Between gasps for breath, the Doctor called back: 'They're all around us. You know, Chesterton, they have an extraordinary range of movement for plants. Quite extraordinary.'

'This isn't the time for a botany lesson, Doctor,' Ian objected. 'All I'm interested in is that we'll be safe once we get inside the cave.'

As he spoke, he crossed the threshold, and gently lowered Vicki on to the ledge there. The Doctor backed in after him, slashing with the light stick, as though fencing with a musketeer.

'Chesterton,' he commanded, 'come and keep watch while I take a look at Vicki.'

Ian glanced around. 'Now where has she . . . Barbara? Barbara!

The Doctor realized that there were just the three of them in the cave, and a frown crossed his features. 'She must be here. Surely she wouldn't have gone out on her own?'

Grimly Ian answered: 'That's what worries me – perhaps she wasn't on her own.' He took one of the light lances from the Doctor. 'You look to Vicki, and I'll just check around outside.'

The Doctor nodded, putting the other rod down. He knelt beside Vicki, cradling her head in his arms. He had been extremely worried about the child; she reminded him very much of his grand-daughter, Susan, his first and dearest travelling companion. Susan had grown and left him, but the loss was very recent, a loss that Vicki had helped to mask. If anything happened to the young child . . . 'That's it,' he murmured, encouragingly, as Vicki began to stir. 'Come along now, come along.'

Vicki's eyes flickered open, and then focused on the Doctor. As soon as she realized what she was seeing, she gave a cry of panic, and tried to move away. Puzzled, the Doctor moved forward. Vicki threw back her head and screamed.

11

To The Death!

Ian was looking about for tracks outside the cave when he heard Vicki scream. Immediately, he dashed back inside. There was nothing threatening there – merely the Doctor bending over her. 'What is it?' Ian asked, worried.

Pushing past the Doctor, Vicki ran across to Ian and held him tightly. 'Oh, Ian, it's you! When I saw . . . it *must* be the Doctor, or you wouldn't be with him.'

'What on earth are you talking about?' Ian asked, completely bewildered.

Vicki wiped her nose on her sleeve, and tried to smile. 'I'm sorry I acted like that,' she said to the Doctor, 'but when I saw you, I thought you must be the robot.'

'Robot?' the Doctor repeated. 'My dear child, neither of us has the faintest idea what you mean.'

'There's a robot,' she explained. 'The Daleks made it. It's exactly like you.'

'A robot that looks like me?' The Doctor couldn't quite believe it.

'Exactly like you, in every detail.' Vicki looked at them, and could see that the two men were wondering if she was quite in her right mind. 'When the TARDIS took off, I snuck into the Dalek ship and hid. The Daleks made a copy of you, to infiltrate our party. Infiltrate and kill, that's what it said.'

'So that's it.' The Doctor looked at Ian, worried. 'This is serious. Barbara would never have left this cave – unless you or I had suggested it.'

Ian realized what the Doctor was getting at. 'Or a robot

that *looked* like you. We've got to find her, and quickly.' He ran from the cave, into the night.

'Chesterton, wait!' the Doctor called, futilely. 'Ah, there's no point . . . This is the time for action, not words.' He returned to Vicki. 'Do you feel well enough to move?'

Vicki nodded. 'And I'm going to stay close to you, so I know who the real Doctor is.'

Smiling affectionately at her, the Doctor handed her a light rod. 'Come along, then, child. Pray that there's still time to save Barbara!'

Barbara had not been at all reassured as she had set off into the forest with the Doctor. He seemed so *strange*, but she put it down to his having seen Ian killed, and his sense of loss over Vicki. Yet, even making those allowances, he was still behaving very oddly. Barbara peered through the gloom, frantically brandishing her light stick if she heard any noises from the vegetation. She could barely see the Doctor, who was scouting the way ahead.

'Is there anything there, Doctor?' she called, anxiously.

After a moment, he said, 'No . . . No, I don't think so.'

'Then hadn't we better be moving on?' Barbara asked. She kept her mind fixed on rescuing Vicki; it made the pain of losing Ian seem a little easier to bear.

'I think we'll stay here,' the Doctor answered, coming back towards her. 'Yes, this place will do very nicely.'

'But I thought we were going to get the Dalek time machine!' Barbara couldn't believe that the Doctor was simply going to stay out in the forest at night.

'Mmm? Oh, there's no need for that, Barbara.' The Doctor was almost up to her, and in the light from her rod, Barbara could see that he looked like a hawk that had just seen a wounded pigeon.

'Why are you looking at me like that?' she asked, backing away. Somehow, the Doctor frightened her, with that eager expression on his face. Abruptly, she noticed that he didn't have his light stick, and yet apparently had no trouble seeing in the dark. What was happening?

'Barbara! Barbara!'

The yell had come from quite close in the trees, back in the direction from which they had come. Barbara's heart soared as she heard the familiar voice.

'That was *Ian*!' she exclaimed. 'You lied to me, Doctor. You *lied*. Why?'

The Doctor didn't answer. Instead, he simply advanced towards her again. Barbara continued to back away from him, waving her rod at him. She took a deep breath and screamed out Ian's name.

'First you,' the Doctor said, extending his arms. 'Then the others.'

As Barbara moved backwards, one of the tendrils from the vines snatched at her feet. As she felt the sharp whipsaw, Barbara cried and stumbled. The Doctor moved far faster than she imagined he could, and pounced at her. His arms shot for her throat, but Barbara dropped her rod, grabbing his wrists. His strength was incredible, and she could barely even slow his attack. His hands were almost on her throat when Ian ran up behind the Doctor. Swinging his rod, Ian dealt the Doctor a blow to the head that sent him flying aside. Without apparent pain, the Doctor rolled over, glared back at them, and then ran off into the jungle.

Before Ian could follow, Barbara clambered to her feet and gripped his arm tightly. She didn't want to lose him again!

'What's happened to him, Ian?' she whispered. 'Why did the Doctor try to kill me?'

'That wasn't the Doctor,' Ian answered. 'It was a robot manufactured by the Daleks.'

'A . . . *robot*? But . . . it was so . . . so real.' Everything was getting to be too confusing for Barbara, but one thing was clear: Ian was alive, and she was too glad about that to worry about a robot.

Ian realized that she was scared and exhausted. He placed his arm protectively about her shoulders. 'It's all right,' he assured her. 'It's all right. It won't fool us again. Let's get back to the others. They're just back this way.'

Barbara was happy simply to hold on to Ian, and let him lead the way. Over the course of their journeys, they had grown very fond of each other. Just how fond, she was beginning to suspect from the loss she had experienced on hearing of his supposed death twice so recently.

It was a short walk before they saw another light, and then Vicki, slashing about with it. Ian laughed, and called out: 'Doctor Livingstone, I presume.'

'Ian!' Vicki saw Barbara, and ran over. Barbara could hardly believe her eyes – both of the people she had given up for lost and dead! She grabbed Vicki, almost asphyxiating her in a tight embrace.

'Where's the Doctor?' Ian asked, prising the two women apart.

'He's right behind me,' Vicki said, happily.

Right on cue, the Doctor stepped out of the bushes to the left of the trail. At the same moment, the Doctor also stepped out of the bushes to the right. The three friends stared at both figures – and could not tell them apart.

One of them pointed to the other. 'Chesterton! Don't just stand there – that's the robot!'

The other Doctor spluttered in fury. '*Me?*' he howled. '*You're* the impostor!'

'Then prove it, my dear fellow,' the first Doctor said, smugly. 'There's really no need to lose your temper. Just prove that you are the Doctor – if you can!' He smiled at Ian and the girls, obviously certain that the other Doctor couldn't prove any such thing.

The other Doctor straightened, and gripped his lapels. 'I don't *have* to prove anything.'

'You mean you *can't*,' the first Doctor snapped back.

This was too much for the other Doctor. He raised his cane, and brandished it. 'Why you . . . !' He moved forward.

The first Doctor backed off slightly. 'Look out, Chesterton!' he snapped. 'It's getting violent!'

Ian could see this. Holding his light lance firmly, he moved to stand between the Doctors, staring levelly at the one waving his stick. 'Put that down,' he said, softly.

'Get out of my way!' the Doctor roared, still furious.

'And if I don't?' Ian asked.

'Then you'll get the same treatment as that confounded

109

impostor!' To back up the threat, he brandished his cane at Ian.

The other Doctor moved in front of Vicki and Barbara. 'Watch him, Chesterton, watch him,' he cautioned.

Ian *was* watching him. He had no desire to be brained by either the real or the fake Doctor. The problem was that he still wasn't certain which of them was which. 'You're still insisting that you're the real Doctor?'

'You don't want to listen, one way or the other, do you?' The Doctor had had enough, and whacked at Ian with his cane. Ian parried the blow with his lance, and then riposted. One advantage of having served briefly in the retinue of King Richard the Lionheart was that Ian had picked up some fine sword-fighting techniques. The Doctor – real or robot – was hopelessly outclassed. In a second, his stick went spinning. Ian poised, ready to make the final blow with his lance. Yet, he was still uncertain.

'Chesterton!' the other Doctor called. 'Now's your chance – destroy it! I know it *looks* like me, but it's just wires and electronics. Destroy it!' Ian still hesitated, so the Doctor added: 'You have to defend us! Barbara and Susan are relying on you!'

'What did you say?' Barbara grabbed at the Doctor. 'What did you say?'

'What do you mean?' the Doctor asked, confused.

'You said *Susan*!' Barbara exclaimed.

'Of course I did.'

'Ian!' Vicki cried. 'That's not the robot – *this* one is!'

At the cry, Ian turned, his rod held ready. The robot, realizing that it had somehow made a mistake, turned and ran into the undergrowth. The real Doctor picked up his stick, and he and Ian set off after the fake.

This time, the robot was the one facing the problem. Since it had no light stick, the native plants did not get out of its way. It was forced to plough straight through anything that was in its path. Having infra-red vision didn't help when fighting a jungle. In a matter of moments, it heard Ian and the real Doctor close behind. Faced with little alternative, the robot spun and raised its cane.

Ian was about to come at it with his light stick, but the Doctor gripped his hand.

'This is *my* fight, Chesterton,' he insisted. Raising his own walking stick as if in salute to his opponent, he then stepped forward and struck. The robot parried the blow, recovered, and struck back. The Doctor whipped his stick into the path of the blow, and then closed in.

Vicki and Barbara arrived, panting. In the light of the three alien rods, the travellers could see two identical Doctors laying into one another with their sticks, each violently seeking to brain the other.

'We've got to help!' Vicki cried.

'How can we?' Barbara asked, practically. 'We can't tell them apart.'

'So how did you, back there?' Ian wondered.

Barbara smiled slightly. 'The robot called Vicki *Susan*.'

'Susan?' Ian considered it for a moment. 'Of course! Both of the previous times we met the Daleks, Susan was with us. And Vicki looks enough like Susan for the Daleks to assume that she still was the same girl!'

The fight came to an abrupt conclusion as they watched. One of the Doctors caught his opponent a vicious blow to the head, and then slammed the silver head of his cane down on to the chest of his fallen foe. The Doctor on the forest floor didn't rise again. The victorious Doctor straightened up, pulled his handkerchief from his pocket, and mopped his forehead.

'Most enervating,' he muttered. He turned to face three pairs of anxious eyes. 'Oh, relax. It's really me this time.'

Nervously, Vicki whispered: 'How . . . how can we be sure?'

'Mmm?' The Doctor looked as though the thought had not occurred to him. 'So I'm to be tested again, eh? Well, would the Daleks know that Chesterton was dubbed Sir Ian, Knight of Jaffa, by Richard Coeur de Lion? Or that you, Vicki, led a revolution on the planet Xeros? Or that Barbara escaped with the Menoptera from the Crater of Needles?' He waved his stick at the fallen figure. 'And if *that* doesn't convince you, then perhaps this will.'

The figure had been broken by the blows the Doctor had dealt it. In the light from the rods, the travellers could see that wires and electronic parts had been exposed.

The Doctor patted each of them on the arm. 'Now, my friends, I think it's high time we returned to the cave. We could all do with some rest. Especially me – I'm not as young as I once was.' Abruptly, he broke into a youthful smile. 'But it's nice to know I can still hold my own in a fight, eh? Even if it was against myself.' Chuckling to himself, he led the way back through the night.

The Patrol Leader stopped in front of the TARDIS. Another Dalek halted behind him. 'The enemy time machine,' the Leader grated. 'With this in our control, they cannot escape.'

A third Dalek, from one of the patrols, arrived. 'There is no trace of the humans.'

'And the robot?'

'Contact has been lost.'

The Leader considered. They had had a number of skirmishes with the native fungoids and other plant life. Their inner power packs were running low. 'Organize a full-scale search of the jungle as soon as it is light,' it ordered. The sunlight would recharge their solar panels. The energy might be needed. The Doctor and his accomplices were proving to be more trouble than had been anticipated.

'I obey.' The third Dalek moved off.

The Leader turned to the other Dalek. 'Remain on guard, in case the Doctor returns.' It then moved back to the time machine. The Dalek Prime would have to be notified of the progress. It was a report that the Leader preferred not to have to make. Again it was of failure.

Ian sat in the cave mouth without a light stick. He didn't dare advertise his presence to the Daleks, wherever they might be. As he sat there straining his eyes to see in the darkness, he could hear the sounds of the jungle all about him. Strident cries, deep-throated roaring noises, and the occasional sounds of something crashing through the paths below told Ian that whatever animal life there was here lived and hunted mostly by night. He couldn't blame them – the plants were probably slower in the dark.

In many ways, this was a terrible planet. It was literally a world where only the strongest, most deadly predators could survive. Perhaps that was a sign from fate – here, the small party would have to face the Daleks now. It was a case of the survival of the fittest, with the Doctor and his friends on one side and the Daleks on the other. A ruthless world like this was probably the most appropriate place for the final battle.

There was a noise from behind as the Doctor moved to join him. 'Chesterton, you get some sleep now. I've had a little nap and feel quite refreshed. I'll watch for a while.'

'Thanks.' Ian stood up and stretched. He felt bone-weary, and rather envied Barbara and Vicki, both fast asleep in the cave. First, though, he returned to squat by the Doctor. 'Things look pretty bad, don't they?'

Evasively, the Doctor admitted: 'It's not entirely encouraging, my boy.'

Ian gestured into the blackness. A raucous cry was suddenly stifled, and something began to eat. It was better not to see what. 'The Daleks are lurking out there in the jungle, waiting to destroy us. Even if they fail, the fungoids might do the job for them.'

'Yes, yes,' the Doctor agreed, impatiently. 'Yet there is some consolation for us. There must be an intelligent species here. Something put those lights in the jungle. And something made these light rods that have been so handy.'

'I know.' Ian looked grimly at the Doctor. 'But did it occur to you that those *somethings* we haven't met might be more dangerous than the things we have?'

'You're tired, my boy. Get some rest. Only time will tell; time reveals all things.'

Ian nodded, and moved back into the cave. Smiling at how peaceful Barbara and Vicki looked, he settled down near them. He was even more tired than he had thought; within two minutes, he was deeply asleep.

In the entrance, the Doctor sat, staring into the blackness, intent on staying awake. It was up to him to stay awake . . .

The Dalek Leader completed his report into the sub-space radio. There was a pause as the Dalek Prime assimilated the information. Finally, there came a reply.

'You have lost four Daleks, yet the Doctor and his companions survive.'

'Affirmative.'

'Your progress is not acceptable. At the first opportunity, you will pursue and eliminate the Doctor. You must not fail. *You must not fail.*'

'I understand.' The Leader understood perfectly; if the Doctor managed to elude him this time, the Dalek Prime would have no mercy. 'His time machine is being guarded.'

'Yes.' There was a pause, then the Dalek Prime said: 'We have no further supplies of taranium in the Dalek Empire. Yours is the only time machine that can be constructed. You must not fail.'

'I understand.'

The Dalek Prime broke the contact. The Leader considered the matter carefully. The assassination squad was the only hope that the Daleks had to track the Doctor through time and space until further supplies of taranium could be obtained. Since the closest known deposits lay within the Terran Empire, there would be little chance of another time ship being constructed until the Earth had been defeated. The assassination squad must succeed this time – it must!

Despite his good intentions, the Doctor had fallen soundly asleep in the entrance to the cave. His gentle snorings disturbed nothing, but were the signal for activity. In the roof of the cave, a small section opened like the iris of an eye. After a moment, a thin cable emerged. This moved slowly down, flexibly peering back and forth. At its tip was a small sensor. Like a snake, it checked the sleeping quartet, and then moved in for a closer look at Ian. It scanned the human,

114

and then went on. Vicki . . . Barbara . . . and finally over the insensate form of the Doctor. It paused longer with him than with the others, as though puzzled. Then, just as silently, it retreated into the roof of the cave. The iris closed, and all was still again.

With a start, the Doctor awoke. His first thought was that day had broken. His second was a feeling of guilt for having slept while on watch. His third, as he opened his eyes, was of sheer astonishment.

All through the evening and the night, he and his companions had been running through the forest. They had dodged the carnivorous plants; they had eluded the Daleks; they had fought and defeated the robot Doctor. And all of that time, they had missed the most incredible thing. The Doctor clambered to his feet and stared outwards over the forest in amazement.

Above the insane growths of the surface of the planet stood an immense city. Huge legs rooted to the forest floor held it in place. The underside of the city was smooth. It seemed to lead from directly above the cave towards the horizon. About a mile away, the city split into two sections, leading to the right and to the left. This enabled the Doctor to survey the incredible architecture of the place. Towers soared toward the skies; roadways and ramps ran about at all levels. Complexes abounded. The entire city was like a metallic fantasy, an architectural rhapsody, blending art and function. Thin spires gave way to what looked like minarets and prayer towers. Cathedrals of steel led into sections that were mirrored glass, reflecting the sunlight downwards. It was a blending of all the cities the Doctor had seen in his travels that had been built by sophisticated, technological races. The entire place was an engineering miracle.

There was no sign of life, however. No cars, hovercraft, airplanes, helicopters, rockets or people were visible. There was no movement of any kind.

Forcing himself to look away from this staggering sight for a second, the Doctor turned his head. 'Chesterton! Barbara!

Vicki! Wake up! *Wake up*! Come, look at this!'

Hearing his companions stirring, the Doctor turned his attention to the city again. From his inside pocket, he removed the compact binoculars he always carried, and unfolded them. The construction work of the city was perfect. Everything melded into a form of beauty and function. Nowhere was there evidence of decay or repair. Neither – even under this closer scrutiny – was there any sign of life.

'Good Lord!' Ian exclaimed, joining him. 'That was above us all last night? And we had no idea!'

'It's . . . huge!' Vicki whispered in awe.

'Well, Chesterton, I think you'll have to admit that the fungoids couldn't have built that.'

Vicki was still taken by the vastness of the structure. 'It must be thousands of feet off the ground!'

'Quite.' The Doctor smiled cheerfully at the others. 'Come along. We must try and make contact with the beings that live there.'

'How do you plan to get in, Doctor?' Ian asked. 'Fly?'

This was too much for the elderly traveller. 'Chesterton, my dear boy, you are without doubt the most—'

'I don't think we'd get very far whatever way we took,' Vicki said dully. 'Look.'

As the others followed her outstretched finger, they saw what she had seen. Three Daleks were moving through the jungle.

'They're coming this way!' Barbara exclaimed.

'They must have found the light housings in the daylight,' Ian muttered.

'We'll have to make a run for it,' the Doctor decided.

'They'd see us in an instant,' Ian objected. 'There's not much cover from here, is there?'

'Well, we can't just stand here and wait to be found!' Vicki cried.

Barbara was still scanning the forest. She pointed off to the right. 'There are three more over there!'

'They're trying to box us in,' Ian realized. 'They must have a good idea where we are.'

116

'The cliff above this cave,' Vicki suggested. 'Couldn't we climb out that way?'

The Doctor glanced down at the Daleks, then upward at the climb ahead of them. 'No,' he decided, sadly. 'It's too steep. They'd be able to pick us off like flies while we struggled up that path.'

There was only one thing that Ian could think of to save the others. 'I'll make a break for it and try to lead them off.'

Barbara gripped his arm. 'No, Ian!'

He shook himself free of her hold. 'It's your only chance,' he insisted. 'If I can hold their attention for a few minutes, it'll give the rest of you a chance to slip off into the jungle.'

'You'd be in the range of their guns,' Vicki objected.

Ian gestured down the slope to the left. 'There's a scattering of boulders there. If I can make it to those, then I've a fair chance of staying one step ahead of them.'

The Doctor looked out in despair. While they were talking, the Daleks were getting closer. 'I don't like your plan, Chesterton,' he commented, 'but I'm afraid there's no better way.'

'All right.' Ian was glad to have the Doctor's support. They all knew that Ian's chances of escape were slim at best, but at least the Doctor was backing him up. 'Give me about thirty seconds after I've made the break, then get out of here.'

'Where shall we meet you?' Barbara refused to consider the possibility of losing Ian again.

'The closest of the city stilts. We should be able to find it easily enough, even in this forest.'

The Daleks were drawing closer to the cave all of this time. Ian looked out and saw this. 'Get under cover,' he whispered. 'I'm going in a moment . . .'

The Leader turned to its second in command. 'Report!'

'Squad two reports strong perceptor readings directly ahead.'

'Attack pattern,' the Leader ordered. 'Our enemies must not be allowed to elude us again!'

The patrols began to split, gliding through the trees and

growths towards the cave above them. The Leader surveyed the ground. 'Section four will enter the cave. Section two will circle to the boulders. It is the targets' only line of escape. If they attempt to leave the cave, then shoot on sight.'

Section two moved off to cover that avenue. The rest of the squad continued to close in on the cave.

Ian swore under his breath. 'Two of them are moving in the boulders,' he called back to his friends. 'They've cut off all escape.'

'We should have expected it,' the Doctor said, glumly. 'For all of their evil, they are not stupid.'

'They've got us completely pinned down, Doctor,' Ian pointed out. 'There's no way we can leave this cave alive now.'

At that instant, there was a sound from behind them, in the back of the cave. Behind it was a room that was almost blinding in its whiteness. Blocking the entrance was a strange creature.

It was about five feet tall, and as much around. It had a small circular base, from which it grew like a balloon. Its surface was not smooth, but broken into triangular sections, like a miniature geodesic dome. A thin band ran about its middle. On the top of this being was a small arrangement of antennae. In several places across its form, there were discs in motion, several of them quite brilliant. There were no signs of arms, or features. From this odd being came a single word:

'Enter!'

12

The Mechonoids

The travellers looked at this creature with a mixture of awe and suspicion. After a moment, it repeated in its electronic tones: 'Enter!'

Ian made up his mind. 'I don't know what it is, but we've got nothing to lose.'

The others were in complete agreement: with the Daleks behind them, following this being could hardly prove worse. They hastily entered the small room that their . . . host occupied. As they did, the door closed behind them. Then, after a second, there was a slight humming noise.

'It's a lift,' Barbara said. 'We're going up – into that city.'

The Doctor was examining their saviour. 'You rescued us from rather a nasty situation down there,' he said, attempting to start a conversation. The creature gave no response. 'I suppose you're wondering who we are, and what we're doing here, umm?' The being made no movement, and gave no sign that it was even listening to the Doctor.

'I don't think you're getting through,' Ian commented.

Vicki moved forward, and reached her hand out, hesitantly, to touch the creature. As she did so, she gave a yelp of pain, and whipped her hand back. 'It's electrified!' she cried.

'Yes,' the Doctor agreed, thoughtfully. 'No doubt it is discouraging all attempts at conversation. We shall just have to wait and see what it has in store for us.'

The first Dalek into the cave looked about in surprise. 'There is no one here,' it reported.

'Not possible,' its companion replied, entering the cave also. 'Perceptor readings indicated that our targets were here.'

There was only one explanation for this puzzle. The first Dalek turned to the new arrival. 'Subject the walls to seismic detector tests.'

The other Dalek moved forwards. Instead of the habitual sucker-stick on its arm, it possessed a small device that emitted low-frequency sound waves. Scanning with the device, it soon located the small lift-shaft at the back of the cave.

The first Dalek moved in to examine this area. After a moment, it communicated to the Patrol Leader. 'It is required that we penetrate the wall in the cave. Section four must return to the time craft for the electrode unit.' It turned back to look again at the hidden door. 'Wherever our quarry has gone, we shall follow – and exterminate!'

'I think we've arrived,' Ian announced, as the lift slowed, and then stopped. The door opened, and they were looking out into the city itself.

There was a huge open space, stretching for almost half a mile in front of them. There were trees, and neat floral arrangements. Beyond those were the buildings gleaming metallically in the sunlight. The only signs of life were numerous other creatures identical to their host. These were gliding along the pathways, engaged in their own unfathomable tasks.

The being with them slid out of the lift, then waited. Taking their cue, Ian, Vicki, Barbara and the Doctor followed. The metal being led the way through what was quite evidently some form of park. The grass was cut, the plants neatly tended, the trees perfect. There was no sign of neglect, or even of work that needed doing. Whenever the party passed others of this metallic race, the creatures would stop, spin and seem to watch, before they continued on their way.

They left the park behind them, and their host led the way to a tall building. As they approached, a doorway opened. The creature moved aside. It was obviously inviting them

120

to enter. Ian led the way, looking about as he entered the room. As soon as the others followed, the door behind them slid shut. The creature that had led them there then moved away, apparently uninterested in further events.

The room that faced the travellers was quite amazing. It was large and spacious, with a high ceiling. Along the left wall ran what seemed to be a bank of computers, screens and read-outs. The far wall was shuttered, obviously some kind of window. In the right wall was a sliding door, leading off. It was closed at the moment. Various items of furniture showed futuristic designs. A low couch, several comfortable-looking chairs, small tables with lamps upon them. All were of pastel colours – blues, greens and pinks being the most common after the basic white of the room. On the walls hung several abstract paintings. Half-way down the right-hand wall stood the only incongruous item, a ladder leading to a sliding shutter in the ceiling.

Barbara headed for the couch and sat down. After a moment, she smiled. 'Well, they obviously intend that we should be comfortable.'

Ian moved to join her, testing the spring of the couch as though he were sizing it up to purchase. 'Mmm, yes, not bad.'

'I don't like it,' the Doctor announced, glowering around the room as a whole.

'Why ever not?' Vicki asked, gently. 'It's clean and comfortable, and those robots seem friendly enough.'

'Yes, yes, the *robots*,' the Doctor stressed. 'Have you not noticed something very singular about this place, um?'

'Such as what?'

'We've seen *only* those robots,' the Doctor observed. 'No animal life, human or otherwise.'

Ian stood up again. 'That's true,' he said, realizing what the Doctor was getting at. A robot force of the size and efficiency of the one that they had seen suggested a large population for them to be serving. So where was everybody?

Right on cue, the door to the other room opened. Standing in the doorway was a young man in his late twenties, obviously very human. He had blond hair, expertly trimmed,

121

and was dressed in a one-piece outfit with what were obviously military flashes of some kind unknown to the travellers. As he paused in the doorway, his face showed a number of emotions flickering past: surprise, disbelief, hope, and then a great grin spread across his handsome features as he bounded into the room, hand thrust out.

'You . . . you've come at last!' he cried, wringing Ian's hand. 'I'd given up hope,' he added, shaking Barbara's hand. 'I never thought I'd see another human being as long as I lived!' he confided to Vicki. 'I can't tell you what all these years alone have meant,' he added, pumping the Doctor's reluctant arm heartily.

The four friends were taken aback – as much by the stranger's enthusiasm as by their surprise at seeing him. He looked at their astonished faces for a moment, and then caught himself.

'It's been so long, I'm forgetting my manners,' he apologized. 'My name's Taylor, Steven Taylor.'

'Steven.' Ian smiled. 'Well, I'm Ian Chesterton, that's the Doctor – Vicki – and Barbara Wright.'

Steven grinned again, and tried to start another round of shaking hands. The glare that the Doctor gave him stopped him in his tracks, and he let his hand fall. 'This is great, huh?' he said, still beaming away. 'I don't know what to say – I'm lost for words! I thought if I ever met anyone again I wouldn't stop talking for a week!'

'And you've made good inroads on that resolution already,' the Doctor snapped. Then, softening, he asked: 'How long have you been here?'

Steven shrugged. 'As near as I can judge, about five years.'

'Five *years*?' Vicki echoed. Barbara shushed her.

Steven nodded. 'I am – was – a fighter pilot. I was off course and had a flare in the main thruster. By the time I recovered, the ship was hopelessly lost, and I had entered this system. My fuel was low, and when I approached this planet – well, the gravity was too strong for me to escape with what little fuel I had. I managed to land – pretty roughly, and wrecked my ship. I wandered around for several days, spending the better part of the time avoiding those fungus things. One night, I saw this path of lights and followed it to a cave. The next morning, the Mechonoids captured me.'

'*Captured*?' Barbara echoed. 'You're being *held* here?'

Steven stared at her in astonishment. 'You think I'd stay here otherwise? I'm just like you – we're all prisoners.'

The concern that the four travellers had felt now solidified. They exchanged glances.

'I see,' the Doctor said, quietly. 'It may sound rather foolish, but we hadn't realized our position.'

'So you don't know what all this is about?' Steven asked. 'Do you?'

Bitterly, the young pilot laughed. 'I've had five years to find out.'

'Then tell us!' the Doctor snapped. After a second, he added: 'Please?'

'Well, as you know, Earth had an expansionist phase a couple of hundred years ago.' Steven assumed that his listeners were from his time period, not realizing that they were travellers in more than the dimensions of space. 'The Government decided to open up this arm of the Galaxy, and sent out a fleet of ships to terraform any marginal planets. This place was one of them, and the shipful of colonizing robots came down to clear the landing sites, start building and generally make things as perfect as they could for the colonists.'

'Didn't they arrive?' Vicki asked, unable to stay quiet too long.

The Doctor glared down his nose at her. 'If you give the young man a chance, I expect he'll tell us.'

Steve winked at Vicki. 'No, they didn't come. Earth got into the Draconian conflict, then the Third Dalek War. That ended the population expansions problem pretty drastically, and this arm of the Galaxy was promptly forgotten. I guess everyone figured that the robots – the Mechonoids – would run down, or wear out or something. No one was really all that bothered.'

'But they didn't run down,' Barbara realized.

'No. When one of them ever shows signs of mechanical failure, the others repair it. This world has terrific metal deposits, which the Mechonoids have mined. They're programmed to repair one another. Now they live here, just like a race of people. They built the city, and tend it carefully. They even water the flowers and weed them, you know. They're waiting for the immigrants to arrive – colonists who will never come.'

Ian thought a moment. 'But why did they take us prisoners, then?'

'Yes,' Vicki added. 'For all they know, *we* might be the first of the colonists.'

'No, you don't understand.' He led them to the screens on the left wall. One was a computer screen that he powered up. Hitting the keyboard, he fed in a string of commands. After a second, the screen lit up redly. It then said, in large letters: 'Password needed.'

'That happens all of the time,' he told them. 'The Mechonoids would be formidable foes if some alien race landed here before the humans. So they have some inner code that Space Central must have known two hundred years ago . . .'

'But which neither you nor we know now,' the Doctor finished. 'Of course, of course. So if anyone else were to land who did not know the right codes, the robots would treat them as hostiles – and lock them up.'

'Exactly,' Steven finished, bitterly. 'Just as long as we're friendly, they keep us here. Perhaps we're specimens for the colonists to interrogate. I think it's just because I've given them some form of purpose they were lacking. They give me everything I want – except the only thing I really desire: my freedom.'

'And if we try to fight our way out?' Ian asked.

Steven looked at him in pity. 'At the first signs of violence towards them, the Mechonoids were programmed to destroy their attackers . . .'

'Sorry I asked.'

Two Daleks entered the cave. Between their arm grips, they carried a large ball-like apparatus. This had several

124

projections and a stand. The Daleks positioned the device so that the largest array of levers was pointing at the hidden lift shaft.

'Electrode unit prepared,' one of them announced.

'Operate,' the Patrol Leader ordered.

The two Daleks began to work the device. Studying the small read-out screen, they manipulated the various projections, setting up an intense, directional electron beam. The idea was to cut down through the Mechonoids' control of the lift, and then use the over-ride device to bring the lift down the shaft. The electrode unit began to hum, and as the Daleks tuned it, the whine increased in frequency. After a few moments, the Daleks could hear the sound of the lift descending.

The Patrol Leader turned to the Daleks that remained. With the destruction of the four during the chase, there were now an even dozen. 'By taking the humans,' the Leader stated, 'the Mechonoids have forced us to take action against them. We will invade their city.'

The scientist commented: 'Skaro reports that they have many powerful weapons.'

'The orders of the Supreme Dalek are that the humans are to be pursued and exterminated.' The Leader surveyed the group. 'The Mechonoids must not be permitted to stand in our way. We will attack!'

At that moment, the hidden lift door opened, revealing the gleaming white room. One by one, the Daleks filed into it. All had their weapons primed and ready for whatever might await them.

In the room where the travellers and Steven were being kept, the five of them were getting nervous. From time to time, the shutters at the end of the room would swish open, to reveal a corridor, and two Mechonoids. It was impossible to be certain, but it appeared as though they were examining their captives. Since the Mechonoids all looked alike, they could never be sure whether it was the same pair, or different ones each time the shutters opened. After the fifth time, Barbara lost her composure.

'Why do they keep staring at us like this?' she yelled. 'Watching everything we do!' She rushed to the window, and pounded on it. 'Go away! Leave us alone! Why won't you leave us alone?'

Steven crossed to her, putting his hand on her shoulder. 'Take it easy,' he advised. 'You'll get used to it. I have.'

Barbara turned her back on the window, trying to blot the sight of the sentient spheres from her mind . . . 'I'll never get used to those things standing and staring . . .'

'Why don't you go into the sleeping quarters?' he suggested, pointing to the door. 'They can't watch you there. You know, for the first month, I didn't come out. Eventually I got so bored that I actually welcomed them watchimg me – at least it gave me something to do.'

Dully, Barbara nodded, and crossed to the door. Ian caught Vicki's eye, and nodded for her to follow Barbara. Vicki understood, and did so.

When the three men were alone, Ian turned to the Doctor. 'Barbara's still shaken from that meeting with the robot duplicate of you,' he said, in her defence.

'Duplicate?' Steven asked. 'Just how did you four get here anyhow?'

'No time for that now, young man,' the Doctor said, briskly. He had been fiddling with the computers, but his knowledge of breaking binary codes was not what it used to be. He was getting very tired of demands for passwords that he couldn't supply. 'We've got to think of a way of escape.'

'That's not too difficult,' Steven answered, casually.

'We can get out of here?' Ian asked, pleased.

'We can get out.' Steven's face showed no enthusiasm for the idea. 'But out to what? I spent two nights in that jungle. Never again. I'd sooner stay here for the rest of my life. There are worse things than captivity.'

'We wouldn't have to stay in the jungle,' the Doctor told him. 'There are two time machines out there. One is mine, the other belongs to the Daleks. If we could reach either of them, we'd be safe.'

'*Time* machines?' Steven asked, incredulously. 'Oh, come on! I can't believe that!'

126

'Young man,' the Doctor said, irritated, 'I really don't *care* what you can or cannot believe right now.'

Steven examined him for a moment, and then shrugged. 'Well, if there really is a chance of getting off this planet, I'll try anything. Even a . . . time machine.'

'Then you know a way out?' the Doctor persisted.

'You see that ladder over there?'

Ian crossed to it, and stared upwards. 'Where does it lead?'

'Up on to the roof of the city. I'm – *we're* – allowed up there any time. For light and for exercise. There are no guards up there, and nothing to hold us back.'

There had to be a catch. 'Aren't they worried about our escaping?'

'No. That roof is half a mile above the ground. Why don't you go up and have a look?'

'I think I will.' Ian gripped the rungs, then looked back. 'Coming, Doctor?'

'Yes, of course, of course. If you'll just lead the way.'

As Ian started up the ladder, Steven called: 'See if you can figure a way down. If you can't, I'll be happy to tell you how.'

'Thanks,' Ian said, dryly. It looked like the young man was attempting to prove he was still the one with the experience here. Ian pushed aside the roof hatch, and clambered out.

The roof was flat at this point, leading to blank metal walls in three directions. The fourth opened up to the sky. There was a bit of a wind, whipping at Ian's hair as he crossed the roof.

'Careful, Chesterton,' the Doctor warned, poking his head out of the hole like a jack in the box.

Ian nodded, and dropped to his hands and knees. Carefully, he crawled to the edge and looked down. Talking about half a mile made it sound so simple. Looking down the two thousand odd feet was another matter entirely. Ian felt giddy just staring down the drop. In the far distance, the tops of the jungle growths could be seen. Ian surveyed the scene. The closest of the legs was a good five hundred feet off in one direction, and at least a thousand feet in the other. The wall down seemed to be smooth for about thirty feet, and then there was nothing till the tops of the trees. He could see absolutely no way to get down, short of jumping – and then the problem would be stopping . . .

Backing away from the edge, Ian shuddered at the thought. 'I can see why the Mechonoids aren't worried about us coming up here,' he commented to the Doctor, who was leaning on his stick and peering over the edge.

'And yet that young man – Steven, is it? – thinks he knows how we can get down.' The Doctor straightened and backed away from the edge with Ian.

'I wish I did.'

'You might,' the Doctor smiled, 'if you had five years to work it out.'

'I can' think of a quicker way,' Ian replied, not relishing the idea. 'Let's go back and ask him . . .'

Down below, Steven was lost in his thoughts. He was still having difficulty adjusting to there being other humans on this planet with him. The possibility of escaping from the Mechonoids had tormented him, day and night, for five years. Yet now it was here, he was suddenly afraid. What did he know, after all, of these four new arrivals? They *seemed* nice enough, and genuine. Yet, if they really did have a time machine – absurd as it sounded – how come they were trapped here with him?

Could he trust them? He had no doubt that they were genuinely what they claimed to be, but just how reliable would they be in a tight situation? An old man, two women and that cynical younger man? Dare he place his future in their hands? On the other hand – could he just stay here and let them attempt an escape without him?

As these thoughts passed through his mind, he was suddenly aware that he was being watched. He glanced up, and saw Barbara and Vicki emerging from the other rooms. 'Feeling any better?' he asked.

'Yes.' Barbara smiled at him. 'I'm sorry I acted the way I did.'

'Well, it was pretty unnerving for me at first,' Steven confessed.

Vicki looked about. 'Where are the others?'

'They went up to—' Steven began, looking at the ladder. As he spoke, Ian reappeared, and dropped to the floor. 'They're back.' The Doctor took the rungs down more sedately.

Ian looked over at Steven, then shrugged. 'It looks pretty escape-proof to me,' he confessed.

Nodding, Steven felt more relaxed. These four worked like a team, each complementing the weaknesses of the others. He had felt rather useless at first. Now, certain that he had an advantage over them, he was happier. 'The first thing you have to realize is that this whole city is run on electrical power. They generate it from vast solar panels on the highest buildings. This operates everything.'

'Like the lights we saw in the jungle?' Vicki suggested.

'Yes,' Steven agreed. 'Well, after I'd been here about a year, I found that one of the main supply cables leads along the edge of the roof. It goes all the way around, so there's miles of it. Every time I went up top for exercise, I would loosen the brackets that held it just under the rim. Just a couple a day, so the Mechonoids wouldn't get suspicious, you see.'

'Where's all this leading?' Ian wanted to know.

Steven grinned widely. 'Down to the ground, if you want to risk it. The cable could be pulled free in a couple of minutes. It's more than long enough to reach the ground by now.' He looked at their faces, and saw the looks of horror that first crossed them at the thought of it.

'Climb down nearly half a mile of wire!' Ian exclaimed, voicing all of their thoughts.

'It's the only way out that I know,' Steven said, simply.

'It's a chance to get away from here,' Barbara commented. 'We should take it.'

Thinking of the drop that he had seen, the Doctor shook his head firmly. 'No, Barbara, we couldn't. The risk is too great.'

Vicki shrank back against Barbara. Looking up, she whispered: 'I'm terrified of heights.'

'The cable's thick,' Steven said, encouragingly. 'It wouldn't break.'

129

'Let's *try* it!' Barbara exclaimed. She couldn't bear the thought of staying here, constantly watched, whatever she did.

The Doctor glanced at her, then at Ian 'Chesterton?'

Ian looked at Vicki, who was plainly terrified of the idea. 'I don't know,' he said, slowly. 'I don't like it . . . but . . .'

Vicki tried to avoid his eyes, and stared through the shutters, which were open. She could see across the park, back towards the lift that had brought them into the city. As she watched, the doors opened.

What she saw sent chills down her spine. 'Daleks!'

13

The End of the Hunt

'That settles it!' Ian said firmly. With the Daleks in the city, they dared not delay. 'Everyone on to the roof – quickly!'

Steven and the Doctor caught on, and hustled Barbara and Vicki towards the ladder. It was quite clear that they had little time to spare. Ian stared out of their prison as the Daleks began to spread out.

The interference with the lift had not gone unnoticed. The central computer of the city had noted it, and dispatched three Mechonoids to check the malfunction. The patrol arrived as the Daleks were examining the area where they had arrived.

The lead Mechonoid paused examining these new arrivals. 'Stop,' it ordered.

The Dalek Leader spun to face the alien robot. 'Surrender the humans,' it demanded.

This was one point that the Mechonoids hardly had to consider. 'That decision is not open to modification,' the first Mechonoid replied.

Ignoring this answer, the Leader turned to the Dalek with the sensors. 'Have you determined the position of the humans?'

'Affirmative. They are in the building directly ahead.'

The Leader turned back to the Mechonoid. 'If you do not surrender the humans, then we shall take them.'

The Mechonoid sent this back to the central computer, which recognized the threat implied. The computer replied with instructions. One of the triangular panels on the upper surface of the Mechonoid slid aside. A small barrel protruded, and then spat a sheet of flame at the closest Dalek. The Dalek, caught by surprise, exploded, showering burning metal.

This was one answer that the Daleks were used to. The remaining eleven opened fire instantly. In the withering blasts, all three Mechonoids exploded.

Before the smoke and debris settled, the Leader ordered: 'Section two: intercept the humans and annihilate. We will cover.'

Two Daleks moved off, through the cheery grounds of the park. The rest formed an escort, scanning the area as they moved forwards. There was no further sign of Mechonoids for the moment. The central computer was analysing this attack, and preparing a counter to the menace.

The Daleks arrived at the quarters assigned to the humans. One of them fired at the door controls, and the door slid open. Two Daleks glided in.

The room was empty. Scanning, the Daleks saw the open door to the roof. 'The humans are on the outer surface of the city,' they reported.

'We must find a means of access to that area,' the Leader ordered. Even as it spoke, several Mechonoids moved into view, their flame throwers at the ready.

The Daleks scattered, presenting less of a target. The two lines moved closer together, and then the fighting began in earnest.

On the roof, the sounds of the battle were clearly audible. Ian and Steven were at the edge, groping for the wire that was suspended just below. Gripping the thick cable, they began to drag it up, tearing it free from the brackets that Steven had weakened. The Doctor and Barbara took the loose lengths from them, and began to haul it in.

Vicki stood as close to the edge as she dared, her courage deserting her by the time she was five feet away. She could feel herself shaking at the thought of the drop. Her head started to spin, and her palms were sweating. She wiped them on her dress, and took a long, deep breath to try and steady her quivering nerves.

Without glancing up, Barbara called: 'Vicki, come on! Help me with this!'

It took all of her willpower for Vicki to take the final steps to reach Barbara. She kept her eyes fixed firmly on the horizon, not daring to look down for a second. She fumbled, then caught the cable, and helped to reel it in. How Steven and Ian could dangle over the edge fishing for the wire was beyond her understanding.

'Steven,' Ian called. 'Where's the end?'

'Junction box down to your right,' Steve panted. 'It's loose – just give it a good pull.'

Ian clambered to his feet, following the wire. The Doctor accompanied him. Between them, they located the box and cable. Gripping the wire firmly, they heaved on it with all their strength. It snapped free, sparking as it came from the box. The box itself started to smoulder.

'I think we've fused the thing,' Ian commented.

'Well, that's the least of our worries for now, Chesterton,' the Doctor remarked. 'Let the Mechonoids fix it.'

Barbara and Vicki now had the rest of the cable on the roof in coils. Steven had the other end, and began to wrap it about a ventilation shaft to anchor it. Barbara joined him, and they soon had it strongly tied.

Vicki realized that she had little choice but to go through with this. Glancing over her shoulder, she could see into the room they had escaped from. The door was open at the front, and several Daleks were in view. It was down the wire to escape, or certain death when the Daleks made it to the roof. Trying to convince herself that the climb down wouldn't be all that bad, she forced her feet to drag her to the edge. Then she slowly looked down.

It was worse than she had feared. Her head felt light, and she could see that far-off ground swaying. A rushing sound filled her ears, and she felt sweat breaking out all over. Abruptly, her knees buckled, and she started to collapse.

Steven had seen Vicki's faint coming over her, and dashed to grab her. Picking her up bodily from the rim, he carried her back on to the roof. 'She's fainted,' Steven told the others. 'We'll just have to lower her.'

Ian nodded, bringing over his end of the cable. 'Right, hold her steady. I'll get this firmly around her.' He started to work

133

on knotting the cable comfortably but securely about the young girl.

As he did so, Steven glanced up, and sniffed. 'Smoke,' he said. 'Can you smell it, Doctor?'

'Yes. I think Chesterton and I started a fire when we pulled the cable free.'

That was exactly what had happened. As the wire had pulled free, it had sent an electric arc into the other terminals. This had in turn created a surge through the local network. Several systems overloaded, and melted. One was in a disposal area, where cut wood from the parks was stored to be destroyed. This had caught fire, and began a slow blaze.

That would not have caused too much of a problem had the city computer system been monitoring the area. Instead, it was occupied with the continued fighting between the Daleks and its Mechonoids. This in itself had caused much destruction, and the shooting continued.

The Daleks were badly outnumbered, but they were accounting for themselves well. The Mechonoids were unemotionally attacking, but the Daleks' superior skill and fighting abilities were telling. For each Dalek destroyed, five or six Mechonoids were in flames. Each explosion caused more small fires, and within fifteen minutes of the start of hostilities, several raging fires had taken grip of the city. The ventilation systems and electrical conduits were acting like chimneys for the flames, spreading the inferno throughout the city.

On the roof, the travellers finally caught sight of the blaze. Steven pointed back down through the trapdoor in the roof. The concourse outside their room was now crackling and melting in the heat. 'It's spreading!' he yelled. 'We'll have to hurry!'

The smoke was starting to get to them as well. Choking, they lowered the limp form of Vicki over the edge of the roof, and began to pay out their makeshift rope. They had very little time to escape. . .

The Dalek Leader realized that the assassination squad was

doomed. Through the growing smoke, it could see that there were now only two other Daleks left. They had accounted so far for about forty of the Mechonoids, whose twisted metal wreckage littered the roads. Sounds of the fires drowned much of the fighting, and the smoke haze was getting very thick. Survival would be impossible, but there might still be a way to destroy the Doctor.

The Leader retreated to the room where the humans had been kept. There was a computer outlet there, as anticipated. The Dalek extended its arm, then connected with the input. Switching to its internal computers, the Leader tied its guidance systems into the main computer bank for the city. Then it began to work on the over-ride controls, feeding selected power surges down the network.

The battle outside was over. A fresh force of Mechonoids had emerged from a building behind the last two Daleks. In the withering cross-fire, the intruders had been obliterated. There was just the Leader left. The city computer tried to locate the last invader, but seemed to be having problems getting input from that quarter. Strange codes were running rampant in the systems. There was interference of some kind. False figures, incorrect data . . . The flood of information was blotting out the real data being fed from the area. It had to be the last Dalek. The computer ordered the Mechonoids to search, but it was already too late.

The Leader cracked the final codes, and then held them in its mind for a second: the self-destruct sequence. If the Doctor and the humans were still on the roof, this would finish them off. The Leader sent the signal to activate the destruction.

The city erupted in cataclysmic fires. The whole palce was consumed, and the wreckage twisted, melted and then collapsed into the jungle below.

14

Home!

As the city above them exploded, Ian threw himself off the last few feet of the cable. He hit the ground, rolled, and then looked about. He saw Steven, who had been above him by about a hundred feet, flung aside, twisted oddly. He crashed to the ground in the depths of the jungle.

Barbara and the Doctor had already reached Vicki, and were hauling her away as fast as they could. Ian rushed to join them. All about them as they ran debris fell, still blazing. Only the fact that the ground was so waterlogged prevented the entire place from catching fire. The city above them warped, as the legs could no longer bear the uneven weight. The molten fury of the fires buckled the supports, and with an incredible sound, the whole place collapsed, shattering by sections. As Ian looked over his shoulder, he saw the main body of the city crash down on to the place where Steven had fallen. There was no hope for their young friend now.

Finally, when they had fled far enough, they stopped to catch their breath. Vicki moaned, and came around. Like all of them, she was pale, and soot-smeared. She blinked, coughed, and then looked about. When she realized that she was on the ground, she smiled.

'What happened to the Daleks?' she asked.

'Oh, undoubtedly the Mechonoids destroyed most of them,' the Doctor said, as though claiming the credit for this ingenious move. 'The rest must have perished in the collapse of the city.'

'Collapse?' Vicki asked.

Ian grinned, ruffling her hair. 'You really missed something there,' he told her. 'The whole place came crashing down about us as we fled with you.'

'Then we've escaped the Daleks,' Vicki said, with a sigh of relief.

'I think that would be too much to hope for,' the Doctor said, as gently as he could. 'There are thousands more still on Skaro, don't forget. Now they've acquired the power of time travel, I doubt they'll leave us long in peace. They hate us so much that they won't just give up trying – especially after this.'

'Well, we've beaten them this time,' Barbara declared defiantly. 'We can do it again.'

The Doctor chuckled, and patted her arm. 'I hope so, Barbara, I hope so.'

'Let's get back to the TARDIS,' Vicki said, happily. 'I'll bet Steven will be fascin—' She looked around. 'Where is he?'

Ian had been wondering when he should break the news. Obviously the time had arrived. 'He was above me on the wire when the city began to collapse,' he said gently. 'He was flung under the city by the force. It . . . collapsed on to him.'

Though they had known Steven for only a short time, they all felt his loss keenly. Without his help and forethought, they would all be dead now.

After a moment of silence, the Doctor cleared his throat. 'I'm sure we shall miss him,' he said, brusquely. 'But we had better make our way back to the TARDIS while it is still light, hadn't we? I for one do not relish the idea of spending another night in this jungle.'

The others nodded, and the party started wearily off through the strange growths, hoping to come across the path back to the TARDIS.

Steven was not dead. As he had been thrown from the wire, he had fallen on to one of the fungoids. The soft vegetable matter had cushioned his fall, though the predatory plant had been considerably damaged. Not wishing to stay around to see if it would recover, Steven had stumbled away. He felt

137

very light-headed, and there was a terrible ringing in his ears. No, that was *outside* his ears! Giddily, he spun around, to see the entire city collapse into the area he had just escaped from.

He put his hand to his head, and it came away bloody. So that was why he was so dizzy! He needed treatment for that! Where was the nearest hospital? He started to laugh at the thought – probably about fifteen light years off – he'd bleed to death before he got there . . .

As he stumbled through the trees, he saw something that made him certain he was delirious . . . A large, blue container, marked 'Police Box' – *in English*! He crashed to the ground, certain he was dying . . .

It was harder finding their way back than the Doctor had expected. In the end, it was not the TARDIS that the small, tired group found, but the Dalek time machine.

The Doctor examined it with interest. 'So this is what has been chasing us!' he exclaimed, looking over the featureless cube.

'Inside, it's huge – just like the TARDIS,' Vicki told him.

He blinked at her, and then smiled. 'Yes, yes. You know, I had quite forgotten that you've had a trip in it, child. Most interesting. I'll tell you what – why don't you give me a conducted tour, eh?' He offered her his arm. Vicki took it gravely, then smiled. She curtsied, and led him within.

Barbara and Ian stayed outside for a moment. Both of them had the same idea at the same time, and turned wondering eyes on one another. Tremulously, hardly daring to believe it, Barbara whispered: 'Ian . . . we could go home . . .'

'I just realized that, Barbara.'

'Home.' To Barbara, the sound of the word was wonderful. For three years, the Doctor had been trying without success to get them back to London, 1963. The Dalek ship could take them there in no time – quite literally.

'You are sure you want to go?' Ian asked.

'Positive.' Barbara looked up at him, her face radiant at the thought of getting back. 'I never realized until this moment just how much.' She gripped his hands, and asked: 'And you?'

Ian thought back – the school days, the walks in the drizzling rain, driving around London, the drinks in the pubs, the movies on Saturday nights . . . He thought about how nice it would be to put his feet up in front of a roaring fire, and not have to worry about being set upon by alien monsters. He missed the simple things in life the most. The TARDIS's food machine was wonderful, but he wanted to eat fish and chips fresh from the shop, to drink a pint of bitter . . . He wanted to send Christmas cards, and even mark ink-stained homework again. He pulled his mind back to the present. 'Yes,' he replied. 'And we'll most likely never get an opportunity like this again.'

'We'd better tell the Doctor,' Barbara said, firmly. 'Apart from anything else, we'll need his help to show us how the time machine works.'

Hand in hand, they walked into the Dalek craft. They could see the Doctor and Vicki over at the controls.

Despite himself, the Doctor was quite impressed by the Daleks' machine. It had some interesting insights that had never occurred to him – though it was more than his pride was worth to admit the fact. 'A death trap,' he said, solemnly to Vicki. 'A veritable death trap! You were most fortunate to have survived your trip in this . . . this infernal contraption. Look,' he explained, gesturing with his stick, 'It's powered by *taranium*! Talk about unstable elements – and it's just about the rarest substance in the Universe! Why, a setting just a fraction off true could disintegrate this machine into its component parts. Dear me, the TARDIS may be a trifle wilful, but I'll take it over this cobbled-together monstrosity. Typical of the Daleks – to try and achieve flight through the dimensions of time and space by brute force! They lack subtlety and poetry, my dear.'

At that moment, Barbara and Ian wandered across. With a new audience to impress, the Doctor started up again. 'Ah, there you are! Capital! I was just explaining to Vicki that . . .' His voice ran down as he realized that the couple were not paying attention to what he was saying. 'What's the matter?' he demanded. 'Aren't you interested?'

139

'Yes,' Ian replied, totally lost in his own thoughts. 'Very.'

'We . . .' Barbara began, but had to force herself to continue. 'We want to go home, Doctor.'

'Home?' he echoed, aghast.

'You can't mean it!' Vicki exclaimed.

Ian stepped forward, and placed a hand on her shoulder. 'I'm sorry, Vicki – but we do.'

'This time machine is our chance, Doctor,' Barbara explained. 'We know you've tried to get us home, and never quite managed it.'

'But you can't!' Vicki cried in horror. 'This machine is a death trap! The Doctor was telling me how lucky I was that it didn't blow up!'

The Doctor cleared his throat, embarrassed. 'Ah, yes, well . . .' he began. 'I was simply drawing the worst-case scenario, you see. Ah . . . if things were not done correctly. Unstable . . . very . . .' He trailed off. 'If it were set correctly, of course – by someone such as myself – well, then it might be perfectly safe.'

'Quite.' Ian had a difficult time repressing his smile.

The Doctor was taken aback by the request that Barbara and Ian had made. Admittedly, in the beginning, they had been an infernal nuisance – they had forced their way into the TARDIS, following Susan. All because they were curious about her! The Doctor had had no option but to whisk them off into time and space. Now, though, after years together, he realized just how much he had become fond of the pair of them, and how much he had come to rely upon them. Losing Susan when she had stayed behind on Earth had been bad enough; now he would be losing two good friends also.

Or was it just two? With a terrible sinking feeling, the Doctor turned to Vicki. 'And you, child?' he asked, dreading the answer. 'What about you?'

'Me?' Vicki was astonished. 'I don't want to go back to *their* time! I want to stay with *you*! If you'll have me.'

Trying hard to fight back any overt sign of emotion, the Doctor put his arm about her shoulders, and drew her closer in. He wouldn't be alone, after all!

Barbara tried to explain more fully. 'Neither Ian nor I can

begin to say what you mean to us, Doctor. We've changed so much these past few years, since we first stepped into the TARDIS. There's been a lot of trouble, but also a good deal of joy . . .' She smiled, fighting back her tears. 'It's not *you* we're leaving – it's our own time that we're returning to.'

Ian moved to Vicki. 'Cheer up,' he said. 'You had to know it couldn't just couldn't go on forever. Barbara and I . . . well, we miss our silly old time, you know. We want to go home.'

Smiling bravely, Vicki nodded. Then she clasped him, and buried her face into his chest.

It was getting far too emotionally charged for the Doctor. He cleared his throat, noisily. 'Well, come along, come along. I suppose you'll want me to show you how to handle the controls.' He shook his head in mock disgust. 'After this, you two will simply have to learn to get along without my guiding hand, you know.'

He crossed to the controls, followed by the other three. He began to flick switches and set the dials. After a moment, he glanced up. 'When do you want to return?'

Ian glanced at Barbara, then replied. 'The day after we first met you.'

The Doctor shook his head and clucked his tongue. 'I knew you'd have trouble without me to guide you. Think, Chesterton, think! You've aged three years – gracefully perhaps, but you have aged! Look at that tan! No London schoolmaster could pick that up overnight, you know. No, no, that won't do at all! Not 1963, dear me, no. I think we'll have you land back in . . . oh, 1965.' He set the controls.

'But how will we explain where we've been?' Barbara asked.

'Do you expect me to have all of the answers for you, eh?' the Doctor snapped in mock severity. 'Apply your minds to it! Now, Chesterton, pay attention.' He indicated one of the main controls. 'I've preset your course. Just press this, and you'll be off. Now this—' he gestured towards a red lever '—is the self-destruct switch. You have one minute after moving it to get free of the area. It will be a small, but satisfying bang. After all, you can't leave a Dalek time

141

machine lying around in 1965.' He looked up at Ian. 'Starting control, self-destruct switch. Do try not to confuse the two, eh?'

'I'll do my best,' Ian laughed.

'And there's just one more thing,' the Doctor added. 'When you get home, you may find a need for money. I think you'd better come back to the TARDIS and pick up all of your things. I believe your wallet and purse will be among them, you know.' He shook his head. 'Really, do I have to do *all* of your thinking for you?'

The journey back to the TARDIS was a fairly swift one. The Doctor left the main doors open while he and Vicki helped Barbara and Ian to pack up their souvenirs and belongings. Finally, they returned to the Dalek time ship. After another round of goodbyes, Ian and Barbara entered the ship with their boxes.

Vicki held on to the Doctor. As they watched, the time machine vanished . . .

Steven came to, his head still a blazing mass of pain. That strange box was still there, with its door open. He had thought it a hallucination, but perhaps it was real? Staggering to his feet, he stumbled forwards, collapsing over the threshold. Then he was convinced he was hallucinating.

It was huge inside, like some sophisticated control room. He couldn't think straight, but he remembered the Doctor claiming to have a time machine. Could this be it?

He managed to rise to his feet and falteringly cross to the control panel. Weak at the knees, he clutched at it for support. There was a door at the end of the room . . . leading where? Just how big was this impossibility, anyhow?

There was a noise from outside. People? Friends? Enemies? Steven couldn't be sure, but whoever it was, he didn't want to face anyone until his head was working properly. He headed for the far door, more falling than walking, and once through it, he spotted a side room, with a bed in it. The thought of rest was too attractive to deny, and he allowed himself to fall finally, into the softness it offered. He was unconscious in seconds.

*

London hadn't changed much in three years. Ian and Barbara hastily fled the time machine, to find themselves in an abandoned garage. Taking their belongings, they walked outside into the fresh air. Behind them, they heard a muffled explosion. Their decision was irrevocable – and neither of them regretted it a bit.

They deposited their luggage at King's Cross Station, and then set off to sample the delights of home, in a dizzying, almost drunken, whirl. They had a pint in a pub by the Thames. They fed the remains of a sandwich to the pigeons in Trafalgar Square. Ignoring the puzzled expressions of the passers-by, they ran through St James's Park, and looked at Buckingham Palace as though for the first time.

'Home!' Barbara exclaimed, happily.

'Well, almost,' Ian said. 'Let's take a bus, eh? Beats a TARDIS for reliability any day.'

They hopped on to the first one they found, and settled down, still bubbling over. The conductor came over and looked at them, waiting.

'Er . . . two threes, please,' Ian asked, extending a shilling.

'Two *threepennies*?' the conductor asked. 'Where you bin, mate – on the Moon?'

He couldn't understand why both passengers broke down, laughing.

Later, after they had sobered up somewhat, Ian and Barbara considered their situation. Three years away . . .

'Good job I own my own house,' Ian pointed out. 'I'll bet your landlady relet your flat years ago.'

'I hope so,' Barbara agreed. 'I'd hate to find I've three years' back rent due!' Then she giggled. 'I'll bet you've got some dusting to do!'

'Be serious,' Ian complained, with a grin. 'I wonder what Coal Hill School looks like?'

143

'Do you suppose we can get our jobs back?' Barbara wondered. 'Hey – I just thought! What are we going to tell the headmaster?'

In the TARDIS, the Doctor switched off the Space/Time Visualizer at this point. Grumpily, he looked around. The control room seemed so much emptier now that there was just him and Vicki in it. It wasn't the same without Barbara and that impudent wretch, Chesterton.

'Hah!' he exclaimed. 'Why should I miss *them*? Always fussing and bothering and getting in my way! Come to think of it, I would have *asked* them to leave. I would! Yes, yes – that's *exactly* what I would have done.'

Still muttering to himself, he crossed to the controls. Slamming the levers and dials, he started up the time rotor. It began its steady rise and fall, as the TARDIS faded out from the surface of Mechanus. The Doctor turned and glared at Vicki. 'I'm quite exhausted,' he informed her. 'I'm going to lie down for a moment. Yes, just a moment. Don't touch anything.'

He hurried from the room, but not before Vicki had seen the tear on his cheek that matched the one running down her own.